SUBURBAN LEGENDS

Marie Andrews

DEDICATION

For Jeff, the living anachronism, and the knight of my heart.

CONTENTS

ACKNOWLEDGMENTS

Heartfelt gratitude to Lani and Emily . . .

. . . and, I suppose, to Jeremy as well.

This is all your fault, you know.

Cover Art by Aidyn Martin

ALTER-ATIVE MEDICINE

Ashleigh sipped her organic herbal tea and squinted at her laptop screen, glowing brightly in the darkness. It was past one in the morning, and she was still hard at work researching at her tiny desk in the front room. She was glad Kyle was still sound asleep in the bedroom since he had to go to work in the morning. She could hear his gentle snores coming from the bedroom even now.

The forum went on for a several hyperlinked pages: mostly women, trading questions and tips for increasing your fertility naturally. Ashleigh subscribed to at least a dozen blogs, podcasts, and bulletin boards all geared toward healthy and organic living. When a well-known celebrity recommended steaming your vagina to cleanse from the inside out, Ashleigh had followed her advice. The resulting yeast infection took a few weeks and several active culture yogurt treatments to clear... she figured she must have done it wrong somehow. In any case, it hadn't worked to get her pregnant, so it was time to move on to another tactic.

The text was beginning to blur before her eyes, and Ashleigh yawned widely. Maybe it was time to turn in. All the experts said to eat well, get plenty of rest, and "relax."

1

That was easier said than done when all Ashleigh could think about was what day she was on in her cycle, and how many more days until the next step could be taken toward being pregnant at last. Tomorrow, just like she had done every morning for months, she'd wake with her alarm clock and immediately take her temperature, looking for the slight rise indicating that ovulation was imminent.

She closed the window and her Facebook feed showed from behind the browser window. She scrolled quickly through the feed to see if there was anything of interest before logging off, when something from the Snowbridge Women's Page caught her eye.

> "Hello ladies! I have exciting news! I have decided to become a consultant for Feng Mofa essential oils and supplements! I am looking for some of you willing to host a party and try out my whole line of products. Remember...you get free gifts just for hosting!
>
> Feng Mofa oils are derived from ancient Chinese herbal medicines to aid in balancing chi, calming stress, and helping your body become the healthiest it can be! Let me help you start walking the path to better feminine health!
>
> PM me to find out more!"

It was a neighbor from the next street over, who Ashleigh only knew in passing. Linda Moffitt seemed nice enough, even if she was a bit on the brassy side. She grew lovely roses in her front garden though, and Ashleigh was intrigued by her mention of natural medicines. Women in the neighborhood seemed to give her the side eye if she tried to tell them that they shouldn't be vaccinating their kids due to all the mercury in them and side effects that the media was keeping hushed up. Maybe Linda would be a more friendly ear than they had been.

Ashleigh closed her laptop, sneaked upstairs, and slid under the covers next to Kyle. With a soft sound, he turned toward her and snuggled close. She drifted off to the sound of his gentle snores.

* * *

At 6 am, her alarm went off with an angry buzz. "Urrrrrrrgh" she said as she hauled her tired body out from under the warm covers. Kyle was already downstairs puttering around the kitchen. She had never understood morning people, but at least Kyle didn't expect her to be one as well.

Twenty minutes later, she trudged downstairs, freshly showered, with braided hair and even a little makeup applied. Kyle gave her a smile and a "good morning" kiss on the cheek as he handed her a cup of tea. He was the only one drinking coffee, now. Caffeine hadn't been shown to decrease sperm count, but maternal caffeine intake had proven risks, even before conception. Herbal tea would have to do for Ashleigh.

"What do you think you'll be up to today, hon?" Kyle asked, his speech garbled by the oatmeal he was shoveling into his mouth as fast as possible. He must be running late again. Ashleigh smiled at him and ran her fingers through the hair at his temples: sandy blonde, with a bit of curl to it. She hoped their little one would have his hair.

"I thought I might walk around a bit. Linda—the lady over on Papyrus Drive with the roses—she started a new business and is offering samples. It's some sort of natural remedy thing. I thought I'd go talk to her. Anything is better than living on the Reddit threads all day again." Ashleigh had been a massage therapist for a few years after graduating from college with a kinesiology degree, but she and Kyle had decided that the reduction in physical exertion would be better for her since they were trying to conceive. The free time was nice to have, but sometimes she did get lonely during the day.

"Hm. That does sound nice, honey." Kyle was typing quickly on his phone, most likely answering yet another work email. There was always some odd question or emergency coming his way. He managed the computer systems for a moderately-sized staffing company, and it seemed that not a day would go by that one of the VIPs would need an urgent password reset or an email recovered or...whatever else it was Kyle did for them. She knew his job was important, but Ashleigh did get frustrated at times when it seemed he wasn't really listening to her. She tapped her foot as she waited near the door to see him off.

He kissed her goodbye absently at first, but then she grasped the back of his neck and pulled him in for a real kiss. He kissed her back with a passion that left her a bit breathless. He smiled at her devilishly. "What do you say we go to that Italian place in town tonight for a treat? We could get calamari for old times' sake and pretend that we aren't health nuts who don't eat fried food. What do you say?"

Ashleigh's lips curved up in a sly smile. "Why Mister Greene, I do believe you are trying to corrupt me. I accept." They shared a laugh, and a last kiss, and Kyle darted out the mudroom door.

As the sound of his car faded from outside, Ashleigh slugged back the rest of the now-lukewarm tea and drummed her fingers on the countertop. She wondered how early was too early to go looking for Linda, then decided she would have another cup of tea first, do her yoga, then head down the street for a little visit.

* * *

4

Ashleigh had to turn sideways to get past the rose bushes encroaching on the sidewalk leading to Linda's front door, and though a branch snagged at her leggings, the heavy scent of roses surrounding her was divine. She knocked on the red door and gave a friendly wave to Will and Ellie passing by on the public sidewalk. She watched them slowly shrink from view, holding hands and murmuring to each other. They turned the corner just as the door swung open.

Linda looked exactly like the kind of woman Ashleigh would have pictured given the name "Linda": she was around 50, with shoulder-length hair that was well-styled. Her clothes were not overly fancy but were of good quality. Her perfume was of a tolerable scent but was applied a hint too heavily for Ashleigh's comfort. She held a mug in her hand with "Everything I Touch Turns To SOLD" printed on it in gold lettering.

"Well, hi...uh, Ashleigh, right? How are you doing today?" Linda seemed surprised, but not upset, at the sudden intrusion.

"Hi Linda. I'm sorry to bother you, but I saw your post on the Women's Page last night and was wondering if you could tell me a bit more about your oils? Do you have a minute to talk today? Right now, maybe?"

"Oh, sure honey. I have a closing at 10 this morning—the old Pevensie house over on Lantern Circle—but I'm pretty free until I have to leave for that. Come on in!" Linda stepped back to allow Ashleigh to enter. "Pardon the mess, I've got a ton of boxes that just arrived on the slow boat from China. At least now I have plenty of samples for my clients, though!" Linda strode through the house into the kitchen, Ashleigh scurrying behind. "You want some coffee or anything?" She poured steaming dark coffee out of the kitchen carafe into the cup still in her hand. It smelled wonderful and looked strong enough to strip paint.

"Uh, no thank you, I just ate breakfast." Ashleigh said as they drifted into Linda's sitting room. "I was just wondering if I could talk to you about your oils. I am a huge believer in natural remedies. I think that nature has already given us all the medicines we need; we just need to utilize them correctly. Creating things in a lab only serves to separate us further from the natural world." She sat gingerly on the very edge of the couch; the various parcels stacked upon it digging into her back. Linda hadn't been exaggerating about the boxes; they were literally everywhere. "So, when did you become interested in herbs and oils? I have used a few of them but only for cleaning and such: thieves' oil for bathrooms and to prevent sickness, tea tree to repel insects … that kind of thing."

Linda swept a lounging bulldog off the slipper chair opposite Ashleigh and sat down, crossing her ankle-booted feet and leaning eagerly over the coffee table. "A few years ago! I realized that every time I got a flu shot, I came down with the flu! There is definitely something they're hiding about those shots. And, I credit my hot flashes going away to ample use of a Qingnian oil blend. I feel years younger, and I sleep better besides! Do you know Lili over at the HOA office?" Ashleigh nodded. "She turned me on to it, and now I'm a supplier for the company that makes the Qingnian oil and a bunch of other stuff besides."

Lili wasn't a resident of Snowbridge, although she was well-known to everyone in the community. She was an employee of the management company that ran the development's Homeowner's Association. The residents' high monthly dues paid for all the amenities inside the neighborhood, as well as for Lili to hold court full-time at her office housed in the recreation center at the heart of the development. She kept a small staff there as well, who seemed to exist only to process paperwork and monitor covenant violations. The running joke amongst the residents was that if you wanted to sneeze outside in Snowbridge, you needed to submit a 5-page application and a $75 processing fee first.

"So, what can I do to help you out, honey?" Linda took a sip of coffee and eyed Ashleigh appraisingly. There was a long pause. Linda raised her eyebrows a bit at the silence, but shrugged and sipped coffee politely as Ashleigh put her words together.

"I'm trying...well, WE are trying...that is, Kyle and I... for a baby." The words finally came out, but Ashleigh couldn't look directly at the other woman as she said them. "Do you have anything in your samples that could help me? I have been taking all sorts of natural supplements and twice-daily diatomaceous earth infusions. Nothing has worked. My period is like clockwork, and I seem to be ovulating, but I haven't even had a false positive, and it's been over a year since we started trying."

Linda narrowed her eyes a bit in thought and sipped her coffee again. She looked Ashleigh up and down and smiled slowly. "I think I can help, honey. But there might be some steps involved and you'd have to be okay with a certain amount of risk."

"Risk?"

"Well, you see, some of the herbs and oils I sell haven't exactly been approved by the FDA yet. But, honey, imagine who we can help in the meantime, without the government sticking their nose in any old time they want! It's bad enough that they're sending those contrails at us daily, am I right?"

"A-are they safe? For a baby, I mean?"

"Oh honey, I'm sure they are! They've been using them in China for years. But you know how our government is...if they can't make money off of it they will stonewall you at every turn. And about the baby...these herbs just help you GET pregnant. You can stop taking them as soon as they've done their job. If you need anything after that we can look into a whole different line of my products." She drained her coffee, then placed the mug on the table. "So, what do you say? I've got about a month's supply in stock right now and I'll get online and place an order tonight for another two months' worth, just in case." Linda was already standing up and digging into boxes.

Ashleigh was torn. She really wanted to believe that whatever Linda was selling could finally be the thing that worked for her. She and Kyle didn't have the money for IUI or In Vitro, but Ashleigh didn't exactly trust those methods either. After all, it was well-known that doctors were on the payroll of the insurance companies and therefore should be avoided whenever possible. The idea of doing things naturally was very attractive to her, and although Linda's comment about risk had given her a moment's pause, the moment had passed. "How much?" she asked.

Linda grinned at her, smelling a deal on the horizon. "It's half price for your first month! Only $200 for your pills for the first cycle. And if they don't work that first month, then I'd be glad to talk to you about becoming my apprentice vendor as well. I get all my stuff at 60% off retail! So, are you in?" Her smile widened at Ashleigh's nod. "Wonderful! I take PayPal and Venmo, and of course, cash. Be right back!" She darted down the hall and, from the sound, had started rummaging in the entryway closet. Ashleigh got out her phone and logged into PayPal. If all went well, Kyle wouldn't see the statement until after she was pregnant, and by then she was sure he wouldn't care. Linda's boots came tapping back into the room.

A pill bottle was tossed into her lap. Inside were capsules that appeared to be filled with ground-up leaves of some sort. Or maybe it was dirt? "What is this, exactly?" She held it up to the light.

Linda placed her palms together and bowed slightly, saying "Ah, ancient Chinese secret. Herbs that only grow in the mountains of some remote province that I can't pronounce. You just take one of those in the morning and one at night. You can start taking them any time in your cycle." She pulled Ashleigh out of her chair and led her briskly to the door. "Now, honey, I have to get going to my closing now. Day jobs, they just get in the way of the fun stuff, am I right?" She waved Ashleigh out the door and closed it behind her so quickly that a puff of air buffeted the rosebushes.

Ashleigh walked home and made herself yet another cup of tea. It was early enough to still be called mid-morning, so she took her first dose of the odd-looking pills. They smelled foul; she had to hold her nose to get it down.

An hour later her stomach hurt a little, but some toast helped calm the ache. That evening, Ashleigh and Kyle went out for dinner as planned. They ordered the calamari, as he had suggested. He smiled at her across the table as they reminisced about their first date, where they both had been trying to impress each other and ordered calamari without knowing what it was. They had eaten the whole basket before the waiter explained to them that the delicious little fried rings were actually squid. After dinner, they held hands on the drive home, stealing glances at each other like teenagers. Once home, they fairly raced to the bedroom to make love and fall asleep in each other's arms. Ashleigh woke with a start after midnight, realizing she hadn't taken her nighttime pill. Sneaking down the hall to her purse, she swallowed it dry and climbed back into bed, breathing a sigh of relief.

As the weeks went on, Ashleigh became used to the stomach aches from the morning pill, and she found that the nighttime pill didn't bother her as much since she often fell asleep quickly. She had decided not to tell Kyle about the herbs at all. Like Ashleigh, Kyle preferred natural remedies, but Ashleigh was sure he would have insisted that they do some due diligence into Linda's supplier first. Ashleigh was sure that the delay would have meant being stuck waiting through another "not pregnant" cycle rather than being already on the road to motherhood.

It was a small deception, but it did snag her conscience somewhat. They had been married almost three years now, and in all that time she had never lied to him. Kyle was a nice man who deserved a wife who could help him achieve his dream of being a father. Ashleigh sometimes wondered what she had done wrong to deserve such difficulty doing something that people did accidentally all the time. Her own mother had told her that both she and her brother had been "surprise" babies. Ashleigh would have loved to have that kind of story to tell, but instead she was forced to sneak around and take mysterious pills. The injustice of her situation sent Ashleigh into a funk, and she started taking extra naps between her long descents into online forums about herbal remedies gone wrong.

Her brooding lasted days. It might have gone longer, but for the phone call that came in at three am one night. Her brother had gotten picked up at the bar two towns over for starting a fight over a pool game. "Of course he called me," Ashleigh muttered bitterly to herself as she drove her car over state lines in the dark. "He can't let Mom think he's not the perfect little man, so he needs his big sister to bail him out of trouble...again."

* * *

"You know, just because I'm not working right now it doesn't mean that I am going to always be around to be your chauffeur. Also, you smell like death."

Hunter pulled the lever to lean back and grinned over at his sister from the passenger seat. "Aw, come on, Ash. Where's the love? You're always saying you wish we could hang out more. Well, here I am, baby! Oh! Wanna have breakfast? I would kill for some waffles right now."

Ashleigh sighed and, against her better judgment, took the next exit off the highway and into the heart of the shopping district in town. Despite her initial misgivings, they both managed to eat huge breakfasts at the local IHOP. She had never liked the place before, but for some reason she couldn't get enough of the special: endless pancakes. She drowned them in maple syrup and fairly moaned with pleasure when her third helping arrived in the hands of the grey-haired waitress named Phyllis.

Her brother, for his part, was too busy to notice Ashleigh. He was downing cup after cup of black coffee and devouring the largest omelet she'd ever seen, probably an attempt to stave off the imminent hangover.

It seemed to arrive about 5 minutes before they pulled into the main street of Snowbridge. Hunter started pinching the bridge of his nose and not watching the road ahead. It was a sunny day and people were out in full force. Ashleigh was forced to wave to Will and Ellie, Dennis the mailman, and even Linda out walking her English Bulldog, all the while hissing threats to her brother through clenched teeth. "So help me, if you puke in my car I will end you. I will bury you in that pond at the entrance to the development."

Ashleigh pulled the car into the driveway and closed the garage door behind them. She got out of the car and walked inside without a backward glance. When she came back downstairs with a pillow and sheets to make up the couch, she found him already passed out on their prized Laura Ashley plaid sofa. Sighing, she dumped the linens on top of his prone form and went upstairs to take a nap herself.

* * *

Kyle, as always, was understanding about the situation. He picked up Chinese food on the way home from work for everyone: Kung Pao chicken for Hunter, tofu in garlic sauce for himself, and Ashleigh's favorite vegetarian lo mein.

Kyle handed her the white takeout container and a set of chopsticks, and as she peered down into it the smell of the food hit her nostrils. It was awful...like something had died. She could almost swear that the noodles themselves were writhing at her, a seething, wriggling mass of snakes. Her stomach turned and she fled to the bathroom just in time.

"You ok, baby?" Kyle asked as she returned to the kitchen. "You look pale." He came over to her, his eyes full of concern.

"Yeah, I'm fine. Just my early morning getting to me, I guess." She looked meaningfully at Hunter, then back at Kyle. "You think you could save the leftovers for me? I might just go to bed now. I'm kind of tired."

"Sure! I'll try to hide it from the bottomless pit over here." Kyle playfully punched Hunter in the arm. "Do you want to go on up to bed now and I can come tuck you in in a few minutes?"

"Sounds good, sweetie." Ashleigh gave him a kiss, then, yawning, started up the stairs to the master bedroom.

She never heard Kyle come to check on her. She fell into bed and almost instantly into a dreamless sleep.

It was about 2:30 am when she woke with a start and had to throw herself out of bed: the nausea had struck again.

As she rinsed her mouth out in the sink, a sudden thought came to her. *Oh my God. I was supposed to get my period yesterday. I was so busy with Hunter and his nonsense, I completely forgot.*

Could it be? She stared at herself in the mirror, wide-eyed and pale even in the light from the nightlight plugged in next to the sink.

Ashleigh had purchased a huge pack of pregnancy tests at Costco a while back and stored them in the cabinet above the toilet. She tore open a test, as she had done so many times before, and carefully urinated on the stick. Replacing the cap, she gingerly put the test on her side of the sink and sat on the edge of the bathtub, waiting, as she had done so many times before. It was too dark to see the clock on the wall, but she waited for 300 heart beats. It was easy to count them because she could hear them in her ears.

She walked hesitantly to the sink, and, squinting, held the test up in the moonlight streaming through the bathroom window.

Two lines. There were TWO LINES.

She dropped onto the bathroom floor, shaking, staring at the test. After so long, finally getting the result she had never seen with her own eyes...it felt like a lie.

She crept downstairs and drank the rest of the orange juice in the refrigerator straight out of the carton. Then she went to her laptop and spent a good 30 minutes searching the internet for "false positive pregnancy tests" and "how early is too early?" As anyone who has ever struggled with infertility can attest, there were quite a few results for her to choose from.

Finally, she felt like she could urinate again. She went back upstairs and took another test.

The wait this time was excruciating, but when she finally looked, the new test also showed two lines. She laughed out loud and covered her mouth quickly to stifle the sound. She needed to be quiet and not wake up Kyle.

"Oh, God...Kyle," she whispered. She should tell him the news...when she was absolutely sure she was right. Ashleigh spent the next few hours drinking everything in the refrigerator, then, finally, several glasses of water, taking test after test.

All of them were positive.

She heard Kyle's alarm go off at 5:30. It startled her, and she looked around at the state of the bathroom. Almost a dozen tests were scattered on the counters and the floor, wrappers everywhere. She scrambled to her feet, tossing wrappers into the trash can and gathering the tests in her fists. She was too late, and she had forgotten to lock the door.

Kyle knocked once quickly, then stepped in. He stopped short in shock at the scene: his wife, eyes wild, hair askew, with two fistfuls of pregnancy tests, standing frozen in the middle of the bathroom.

It only took him a moment. He paused, looked her up and down, and then leaned on the doorframe with exaggerated casualness. "You okay, baby?" There was apprehension in his eyes.

She couldn't speak. She just held out her hands and poured the tests out like rose petals. He caught only the last few...apparently even Kyle didn't have good reflexes this early in the morning.

He looked at the tests, then up at Ashleigh. "Ash? What do two lines mean?" His eyes were uncertain, yet hopeful.

She couldn't speak. She could only nod at him as her eyes filled with tears.

He sat down on the bathmat with a thump, gazing at the tests in his hands again. Then, he did the oddest thing ... he laughed.

He laughed until tears filled his eyes and spilled down his cheeks. His head was thrown back against the wall, his shoulders slumped in what could only be called relief.

Then he jumped up, and hugged Ashleigh and spun her around. "Baby! We're having a BABY!" His voice echoed on the walls, a counterpoint to her squeal of delight. He put her down ever so gently, then looked into her eyes.

"What can I do for you? Are you ok? Do you want breakfast? Coffee? No—no coffee. Tea? Juice? The moon? I'll get it all for you."

Ashleigh touched his dear face and sighed. *They had done it. SHE had done it. Finally.* What a feeling it was, not to be a failure anymore. To finally be the wife Kyle needed. The wife that he deserved. "I'm fine. Just a little tired. I might go back to bed if you don't mind. Could you bring me some tea before you leave for work? Maybe?"

"Work?!?" He laughed again, the joyful sound amplified by the tiled floor and walls. His laughter felt like a hug. "I'm not going to work today. I'm here for you, baby. I'm calling in, and I'm turning my phone off." He lifted her chin to look deeply into her eyes. "Now...are you absolutely sure that I can't make you breakfast?"

* * *

It was noon before Ashleigh left her bed. She couldn't remember the last time she had been so lazy. After months of feeling like a failure, as she scrambled for purpose, for meaning, she was relishing in finally feeling useful, worthwhile, and adored.

After a few brief spats with nausea in the morning, Ashleigh managed to eat lunch, polishing off her entire entree from the night before in one sitting. Eating was finally fun again. She had been dieting so long, following weight control plans from the natural living websites. The studies all showed that being on the skinnier side of "normal" was optimal for ovulation. But now that she didn't need to worry about that anymore, she enjoyed the indulgence of eating whenever she was hungry, rather than when the nutritionist websites decreed the correct time for a meal or a snack should be.

Even Hunter seemed easier to deal with. He was amiable, and he didn't tease her once or try to get her to inadvertently smell something weird that might set off the nausea. He dug deep into their freezer and made himself some ancient-looking pizza bagels for a snack. They looked to Ashleigh simultaneously appealing and yet abhorrent. Ashleigh found that today his eccentricities were easier to shrug off than ever. It *must be all those maternal hormones*, Ashleigh thought smugly to herself. *I really should send Linda some flowers or something. Those herbs are a miracle.*

The day continued, idyllic. Ashleigh was surrounded by the caring of her two favorite men everywhere she went and felt the love and adoration pouring in from both sides. Hunter was uncharacteristically considerate and tried to make her laugh. They watched old streaming episodes of

MST 3000 and ate popcorn while adding their own tidbits to the awful movies roasted during the show. It was like the old times, before their father had died, and their mother had become consumed with making sure that Hunter never had a hard day in his life. Ashleigh felt a newfound sympathy for him now, realizing that perhaps he was a victim of his circumstances, too. He hadn't ever asked to be the overprotected youngest child, just like she had never asked to be infertile.

OH! Well, I'm not infertile anymore, she thought with a smile. All right, a smug smile. A smug PREGNANT smile. The smile grew wider. And wide*r.*

"Hey, sis? You ok? You don't look like you're enjoying the show anymore. That face looks more at home terrorizing Gotham than watching reruns of 90's tv." Hunter threw a popcorn kernel at her from the easy chair.

Ashleigh giggled and threw a pillow back at him. "Hey, bro...why so serious?" They shared another laugh. It was so good to be happy again.

Kyle made dinner that night. He hadn't cooked in ages, not since before Ashleigh had quit working. His recipes weren't exactly gourmet: grilled meats, rice, or roasted vegetables, but the decadence of waiting for dinner to be served TO HER for a change was exhilarating.

After dinner, Hunter and Kyle did the dishes while she took a leisurely shower and prepared for bed. Kyle crawled in next to her that night, tentatively. He reached for her, stroked her arm, then stopped as if afraid.

"I don't break, you know." Ashleigh murmured to him. "You can't do anything to hurt the baby, and I've had such a wonderful day." She twined her arms around his neck and kissed her husband deeply. They made love, urgently, and fell asleep in each other's arms. Ashleigh drifted off, sure in the knowledge that this was the start of the perfect life she had always wanted.

* * *

The next morning Ashleigh kissed her husband goodbye and waved him out the door to work. She couldn't stop smiling, watching the blue car disappear around the corner. Then, the smile faded as a sudden bout of nausea struck and she raced back inside to the nearest bathroom.

After the sickness passed, Ashleigh sat on the tile floor and leaned her head back against the wall to catch her breath. There was a gentle knock on the door. "Hey, Ash, you want a glass of water? The door opened a crack, and a hand snaked its way around with the offered drink. She took it gratefully and sipped slowly. His head now poked around the door. "You gonna be ok? I was going to head out soon. I have to go to work today. I can catch an Uber; you don't have to get up."

Ashleigh didn't open her eyes, her head still resting on the wall. "Gee, that's nice of you. I bailed you out of jail, put you up for a few days, and you're letting me off the hook as your work chauffeur too?" The words came out a little harsher than she had meant them to, and Hunter started to turn to go. She sighed and opened her eyes. "Wait, come back. I have to do an errand today anyway; I can drop you off. Can you wait about a half hour for me to get ready?"

"Yeah! Are you sure? Thanks, sis. Love ya bunches." He turned to go again, and she heard him start rummaging in the refrigerator.

"Don't you dare eat any of my snacks!" she chided half in jest as she climbed the stairs to her bedroom. His answering snicker meant he understood that it had been a joke, but she could have sworn she heard him put something back into the fridge, nonetheless.

Ashleigh hadn't been lying; she did have an errand she wanted to do. While she was upstairs getting ready, she messaged Linda and asked to meet up that morning. After dropping Hunter off at work, she pulled into the driveway of Linda's house. The front door opened, and Linda waved her in with one hand, gripping her ubiquitous coffee cup in the other. When Ashleigh came through the screen door, the smell of the coffee in the air hit her and she covered her mouth with her hand, eyes wide. Wordlessly, Linda ushered her into the guest bath nearby just in time.

Ashleigh came back out of the powder room a few minutes later, embarrassed. "I'm so sorry about that, Linda."

The other woman smiled at her kindly and patted her shoulder gently. "Something you wanna tell me, honey? Some sort of news, maybe?" She winked conspiratorially at Ashleigh.

"Uh, yeah! I got a positive test last night... well, a few of them, actually. I wanted to be sure."

"Wonderful! Did you come to tell me a success story? That's really sweet of you honey." Linda sipped her coffee. "But you didn't need to come over for that. Maybe there's something...else...I can do for you?" Ashleigh had to admit it, Linda was shrewd.

"Well, actually, yes." Ashleigh began, sitting on the barstool at the kitchen counter. "So, obviously the herbs worked. I can stop taking them now, right? Because I have to tell you, I'm not sure that there is any way I could swallow those pills right now and keep them down. They taste pretty awful."

"You got it, sugar; you're all done with the fertility herbs." Linda walked over to the carafe to warm up her coffee. "But I've got some new oils for you if you'd like some help with that morning sickness."

Ashleigh's head jerked up and she gazed happily at Linda. "Oh, wow! Could you really? God, that would be great. What do they cost, though? I mean, I'm sure it will be ok with Kyle since I only had to pay for one month's worth of the herbs."

Linda was already moving down the hall to her storage closet under the stairs. Her muffled voice drifted back to Ashleigh. "Tell you what, punkin. I'll give you the first bottle at cost, which is only $25, if you're willing to act as a sort of spokesperson for my oils. I would just need to take a picture of you when you start showing and you can post online about how the oils helped cure your morning sickness." She stepped out of the closet, bumping into Ashleigh who was already there waiting for her, holding the cash in her outstretched hand. They shared a little laugh. Linda pocketed the money, held out the bottle to Ashleigh, and gave her a little hug. "You're going to be ok, sweetie. Now, take this oil and go rest. You just rub this on the soles of your feet each night. You can use a little as soon as you get home if you'd like, as well. It has a really pleasant smell, so it shouldn't bother your stomach."

Ashleigh hugged the woman again, even more tightly, then took her leave and raced home to oil her feet. So far, so good. She managed to eat a little lunch, and once her stomach wasn't empty, she found that she was very sleepy. *It must be the pregnancy*, she thought to herself. *All the blogs say that you're really tired for the first few weeks.* As pleased as she was to be right on track with her internet research, she was happier still to crawl back into her bed and close her eyes. The light scent of the oils (a bit like cloves but mixed with a musky scent she couldn't quite place) wafted up at her from her feet as she settled the covers around herself and closed her eyes.

Ashleigh had the strangest dream. She was painting the spare bedroom for the new nursery and had to open the new can of paint, but when she cracked the lid, the paint can was full of mice. They squeaked and writhed in the can, their pink noses and tails standing out against the grey-brown of their fur. Instead of being disgusted, she reached into the can and picked up a squirming mouse by its tail, holding it up to examine it closely. Even in her dream, it seemed to look at her with fear in its glittering black eyes.

Then, she raised the creature above her and lowered its head into her own waiting mouth. The crunch of its skull between her teeth was so satisfying that she tossed its dripping body aside and reached into the can for another. And another.

Ashleigh started to notice her hands felt cold. She stopped picking up mice and rubbed her palms together for warmth. They were sticky and covered with some sort of grit. In her confusion, Ashleigh opened her eyes, waking herself up.

She was in her kitchen, standing in front of the refrigerator. The carton of eggs that had been nearly full that morning now stood open with one egg left. She gazed with mounting shock and horror at her hands, which were, indeed, sticky. They were covered in raw egg, and there were streaks of both yolk and white dripping down her chin and the front of her t-shirt, not to mention bits and shards of eggshell.

The skulls. In my dream. Oh, God.

Sleepwalking? How odd. Ashleigh had never done something like that in her life, but she had read all sorts of stories about weird things that happened to people when pregnant. She knew that odd food cravings and aversions were normal, as was restless leg syndrome. Why not sleepwalking too?

Luckily, they only bought organic pasteurized eggs, or Ashleigh might have had a panic attack about a salmonella infection. Nonetheless, eating several raw eggs in a row was not a feat she wanted to repeat anytime soon. She changed her clothes, cleaned up the kitchen, and set about making a marinara sauce and pasta for dinner that night. Linda's oils seemed to be doing the trick; none of the ingredients set off her stomach at all.

As the sauce simmered, she stroked her belly and murmured to it "Don't worry, little one. I'll get it together. I'll send down some good food for you soon. You have lots of growing to do, you know." She stirred the sauce with one hand and idly picked up a discarded onion skin from the counter, nibbling as she hummed contentedly to herself.

* * *

She and Kyle had a lovely dinner, and after some coaxing from Ashleigh, he headed to the basement to run on the treadmill. She felt full of energy and happy to nest a bit and clean up the dinner dishes alone.

She stacked the dishwasher and ran hot water into the sink to scrub the pots and knives. As she pumped the all-natural dish soap into the sink to create suds, she was struck by how good it smelled. A bit of the soap dribbled down her finger, and she put it to her nose and inhaled deeply. The scent was delicious. With a quick glance at the basement door and a careful pause to listen that the treadmill was still running, she tentatively put out her tongue and licked the soap off her finger.

It lit up all the taste buds on her tongue. Sour, flowery, and bitter all at once, but also a soft, almost fizzy feeling from the soap itself. She swirled the flavor around in her mouth, savoring it with a soft sigh. When the flavor subsided, she stared hard at the soap pump for a long time.

Her hand seemed to reach out on its own, bent into a claw full of desperate and depraved yearning. She seized the soap dispenser and squirted several pumps directly into her mouth. As she was about to do it again, she heard footsteps on the stairs. Quickly, she replaced the soap and was busily scrubbing a pot when Kyle walked into the kitchen for a glass of water. "Did you have a nice run, honey?" she asked.

"Definitely. I've got to keep in shape if I'm to chase a little one, eh?" He kissed her on the cheek and patted her backside. "I'm going to go upstairs and shower real fast. Are you coming upstairs soon? I'd love to cuddle up to you tonight. I have a beautiful wife and a belly full of pasta; I'm a happy man."

Ashleigh giggled and nodded to him, turning back to the sink. From its place on the counter, the soap pump seemed to be looking at her reproachfully, as if to say: **YOU KNOW WHAT YOU DID.**

* * *

The next several weeks seemed to pass in a blur. Although there were several more short bouts of nausea for Ashleigh, they became infinitely more controllable with Linda's oils. Ashleigh even went back to visit her new consultant/friend and upgraded her wellness subscription to include vitamin supplements that, according to Linda, contained a very special kind of fish oil that would do wonders not only for her baby's development, but keep Ashleigh's hair and nails healthy. Linda snapped several pictures of Ashleigh as her pregnancy started to show, with her turned sideways and holding various bottles of oils and supplements. Lili, the head of the HOA who had brought Linda in as a sales rep, even printed large versions of the pictures as advertisements for the community notice board. Linda's direct sales business grew by leaps and bounds.

By now, Ashleigh had developed a taste for almost every soap in the house, but Kyle hadn't noticed a thing about her new predilection. Since they only bought all-natural soaps, Ashleigh decided she wasn't too worried about it. Every once in a while, there would be a whisper in the back of her mind that she really should look up the side effects of soap consumption, but the simple fact was that the pull was too great at times to ignore. Plus, it was easier to turn a blind eye to any bad possibilities after facing the fear of infertility for so long. She was eating healthy otherwise and gaining weight well. According to her internet research, she was about 18 weeks along now. She had stopped going to her doctor appointments last month when the obstetrician suggested an ultrasound soon. At the time, Ashleigh had gasped and clutched her belly in horror. "This baby is fine! He doesn't need you shooting any rays into his head or making him deaf with the ultrasound. It's bad enough I let you use that horrid microphone for the heartbeat last time. You heard it, ok? Our baby is fine."

The doctor had argued with her, but the longer he went on the more she closed down. He was obviously already bought and paid for by Big Pharma. She told him that she wouldn't take his yucky vitamins that were all made in a laboratory, nor would she undergo his insane glucose test he had ordered. What if she took it and made the baby diabetic? She was sure she'd read an article about just that thing happening. On the way home from the doctor's office that day she stopped by Linda's house and signed up to be her apprentice sales representative for the oils. Everything Linda had given her had worked, and there was so much more to trust there than in what any doctor said. Results were what was important, and Ashleigh wanted to help more women be entrepreneurs (what Linda loved to call "girl bosses") for Feng Mofa, Inc.

After eating a healthy lunch with a good squirt of soap for dessert, Ashleigh took a walk around the neighborhood. The day was beautiful and clear, and there were people playing in the enclosed dog park. A Cairn Terrier and a German Shepherd were barking joyfully at each other while their owners chatted on the bench. Ashleigh patted each on the head, then waved to their owners and walked proudly on, caressing her belly a bit and wondering if they could tell she was pregnant. She hoped she was getting to the point of being obviously pregnant, and not just fat-looking.

She looped the block and went down and around the last cul-de-sac before their street, passing Will and Ellie's house. She paused to listen to the wind chimes hanging on their porch: a huge metallic one whose ring sounded like church bells, and a small bamboo one decorated with an Asian dragon. She heard noises coming from the backyard, so she craned her neck as she followed the curved sidewalk back up the street. They were in the backyard, swinging bamboo swords at each other, bantering and laughing. What a strange way to spend time together, playing at fighting, she thought.

The Japanese maple at the corner of their yard whispered:

I GUESS THAT'S THE KIND OF THING YOU DO WHEN YOU'RE CHILDLESS AND BARREN. YOU'LL BE TOO BUSY TO WASTE TIME LIKE THAT, VERY SOON.

She smiled smugly, caressing her belly again and waving goodbye to the tree. It was time for a snack, and perhaps a nap too. She had earned it.

Ashleigh woke in the middle of the night to urinate...again. After she climbed back into bed next to Kyle, she lay on her left side, like all the pregnancy blogs said to do. She curled her legs up, almost in fetal position, and rested her right hand on the pillow next to her face. Just as her breathing began to slow, it felt as if something was moving against her stomach on the left, on the side touching the mattress. It was just a slight brush, a feeling not unlike when one is in a pool or bathtub and there is movement in the water nearby. If her stomach were a goldfish bowl, it was as if the fish had just swum very close to the glass. Her eyes snapped open, but she didn't dare move. Was it the quickening? Tiny kicks, happening at last? She held her breath, waiting.

Another, stronger this time. Almost like a poke, against the mattress again. Tears filled her eyes as she pulled her legs up close to her rounded belly. He...or she...was awake. "Are you saying hello, little one?" She whispered to the little fish inside her. "Hello."

Kyle was snoring gently, his back to her. She knew she really should wake him.... but at the moment, her feelings were too precious to speak them out loud. Besides, if she jostled too much, the feelings might stop. This caress, this hello, was all for her. She had gone through so much to get to this day. After all the nausea, and cravings, and nighttime pee breaks, here at last was her reward.

The tears dropped from her left eye onto the pillow, while more ran over the bridge of her nose from her right eye to join their fellows. She didn't dare move to brush them away. The wriggles happened a few more times, spacing themselves apart each time. Somewhere in between enjoying the last and waiting for the next, Ashleigh fell deeply asleep once more.

It was a very deep sleep, indeed. Kyle, in an uncharacteristic show of stealth, had gotten up and dressed and left for work without her even noticing. He had even pulled the bathroom and hall doors so that they were almost closed to keep the light from peeking in too much. Ashleigh sighed in happiness. Her stomach growled, and she giggled to herself.

Throwing the covers back and reaching for her robe, she decided to have a slow morning and not get dressed immediately. Ashleigh walked toward the outer bedroom door leading to the hallway.

HEY! WHAT'S THE DEAL, SISTER?

Ashleigh spun toward the sound. The voice had come from the en suite bathroom. She crept along the wall to the bathroom door, sliding her hand along the almost-closed door and, in a show of bravery she might never have expected of herself before, swung it open.

The bathroom was empty.

YEAH, OVER HERE. ARE YOU GOING TO JUST PUT THE LITTLE ONE IN DANGER WITH GINGIVITIS? SOME MOM YOU ARE, LADY. DO YOU EVEN READ MY PACKAGING?

Ashleigh froze where she was, peering through the shower curtain. The voice was behind her now. She turned toward the sink, but again, there was nobody there. Then, she saw the toothpaste tube move. It was propped...no, not propped...it was <u>standing</u> next to the faucet. The tube was bent in such a way that the cap seemed to be a nose of sorts...it was a snake with "Toms of Maine" emblazoned down its side, poised to strike.

C'MON, LADY. IT ONLY TAKES TWO MINUTES. YOU'VE BEEN SLEEPING ALL DAMN MORNING, AND YOUR BREATH STINKS TO HIGH HEAVEN. TRUST ME.

The cap unscrewed itself and fell to the counter. The toothpaste tube was still, as if waiting for her to act.

Ashleigh stood frozen in shock. There was a shudder from the tube looking at her, as it made a noise very much like clearing one's throat. With shaking hands, she picked up her toothbrush and held it out toward the open tube. A grunting sound, like that of someone having a bowel movement, came from it as the toothpaste spurted out onto the bristles. Against her better judgment, and perhaps out of fear or morbid curiosity, Ashleigh wet her toothbrush and started to clean her teeth. When she made as if to spit the foam into the sink, she was treated to another outburst from the counter's inhabitant.

NO NO NO...SLOW DOWN THERE, MARIO ANDRETTI! YOU'VE STILL GOT 21 SECONDS TO GO!

She obediently brushed longer, and when she spit and rinsed her brush at last, the tube bent and retrieved its cap.

SEE? THAT WASN'T SO HARD NOW, WAS IT? NOW, I'LL SEE YOU TONIGHT, LADY, AND WE'LL MEET UP WITH OUR MUTUAL FRIEND MR. FLOSS.

Then, it fell silent and dropped to the counter, an inanimate object once more. Ashleigh backed out of the bathroom and crept out of her room and down the stairs. She was understandably shaken by the experience and found that she now peered at nearly every ceramic knickknack and candlestick on her way to the kitchen. She surveyed the counters there, looking for anything twitching or out of place.

Nothing moved. She sighed and started to relax. Maybe she had been sleepwalking again, and the toothpaste was just a dream, like the one she'd had with the mice. Nonetheless, she opened the door of the refrigerator gingerly, almost expecting the condiments to start singing to her. Vaguely disappointed when nothing happened, she gathered vegetables, soy butter, and eggs to make an omelet for herself.

The morning passed without anything unusual happening, and Ashleigh had started to dismiss the odd incident as a dream. She happily tidied up the kitchen after breakfast, then took a long shower, shaving her legs and even doing a conditioning treatment on her hair...not that it seemed to need it. Her hair seemed even thicker and wavier than before. She felt so beautiful, like Mother Earth. Her energy level was still up, so she took a walk around the neighborhood. There was an odd moment when the Cairn Terrier and the German Shepherd growled at her warningly through the fenced-in section of the dog park, but their owners soon called them away. Ashleigh only noticed the incident because she had always been the sort of person that dogs liked. Could it be her increased hormones affecting the animals? She shrugged to herself and looped around the cul-de-sac again toward home.

Back in her kitchen, Ashleigh made herself a cup of herbal tea and took it to her desk. Booting up the laptop, she scrolled through a few of her favorite blogs. It was more of the same, and she didn't need their advice anymore anyway. Instead, Ashleigh amused herself for a bit scrolling through baby name websites.

The tea, being hot, must have woken the little one. There was definitive squirming in her belly now; there was no mistaking it for gas or hunger pangs anymore. She picked up her mug for another sip, rubbing her stomach with her other hand.

OH, POOR DEARIE. YOU ARE THICK, AREN'T YOU?

The voice came from off to her left, near the bookshelves. Ashleigh's head spun around, and her hand jerked so violently she nearly spilled her tea.

Nobody there. Again. And then, she saw something move. She got up and walked cautiously over to the bookshelves. On it, there was a figurine of a wooden angel, one of those popular gift shop ones with the wire wings and blank faces. It usually stood with its hands entwined lovingly around a long-stemmed red rose, but now it was looking up at her with its blank face, tapping the rose against its palm like an impatient schoolmaster with a cane.

Against Ashleigh's better judgment, she spoke to the figurine, her voice a harsh whisper. "W-What do you mean?"

The angel stopped tapping its rose and shook its head at her sadly.

DOES IT <u>REALLY</u> FEEL THE WAY YOU'D EXPECT A BABY WOULD? DOES IT FEEL LIKE ARMS AND LEGS IN THERE TO YOU? I REALLY THINK YOU SHOULD PAY MORE ATTENTION, DEARIE. WITH ALL OF THE INTERNET AT YOUR DISPOSAL, WOULDN'T SOMEONE HAVE DESCRIBED IT WELL ENOUGH THAT YOU'D KNOW SOMETHING WASN'T RIGHT? I MEAN, I'M MADE OF WOOD AND WIRE AND I CAN TELL SOMETHING'S GONE WRONG...VERY WRONG. YOU'RE IN DANGER. YOU NEED TO WAKE UP, DEARIE.

Its face, eerily blank of features, nonetheless communicated pity and contempt in spades.

Something giggled behind her. The soap pump waved its nozzle at her and giggled again. The angel laughed too, its wire wings jingling softly with the motion. It waved the rose at the soap pump in greeting. The soap called out from its post at the sink.

I MEAN.... SHE'S BEEN EATING SOAP FOR MONTHS. "IT'S ALL-NATURAL", SHE SAYS! WHAT AN IDIOT!

It dissolved into laughter once more and fell onto its side on the counter, rolling back and forth in its mirth.

Ashleigh was horrified, rooted to the floor in the middle of her living room as, one by one, object after object began to laugh and mock her. The throw pillows kept whispering and throwing her sidelong glances, while the art print of a waltzing couple in the rain took a break from their dance to call out insults from under their umbrellas, their servants glaring balefully at them as the rain pelted down.

The woman stuck out her tongue at Ashleigh, then laughed and simpered up at her dance partner.

Ashleigh covered her ears with her hands and started to back out of the room. As she did, the lamp stuck out its cord and tripped her. She fell onto her bottom on the carpet. It wasn't a hard fall at all, but she screamed as she fell out of the shock and surprise of it. The pillows and figurines and even the ivy plant on the windowsill started to creep toward and surround her. She covered her head with her hands and curled into a ball, screaming again so loudly that it tore at her throat and made her ears ring. The scream seemed to go on forever, and the whole time Ashleigh was paralyzed with dread, waiting for the first of the creeping things to touch her.

At last, she ran out of breath and had to suck in air like a drowning man, in vast heaving spasms. It wasn't until she started to be able to breathe in without the loud sounds that she chanced to crack an eyelid and peek furtively around the room. Her eyes went wide as she looked around in earnest.

Everything was as it should be. Nothing was out of place. All the knickknacks and decorations were on their proper shelves. The throw pillows arranged nicely on the couch with their perfect karate-chop dents. The couple were once again dancing in the rain with their faces turned away from her, the maid and butler holding umbrellas high over their heads on the empty beach.

Ashleigh got shakily to her feet, her eyes darting all around like a trapped animal. She bent and looked at the angel sitting on its customary shelf, once again clutching its rose lovingly. She poked at its blank face. It slid backward a bit on the shelf, but it didn't react at all. Her head whipped back toward the kitchen. The soap pump was standing idly by the faucet, as always, its nozzle pointed ready to dispense into the sink at any time. It did not look at her as she picked up her laptop and sidestepped out of the room toward the front door. Ashleigh decided she wasn't staying in this house alone right now.

Something the angel had said was sticking with her. It had read her thoughts and worries as easily as a grocery list. The movements DID feel odd, more like a fish or a squid or something...not like a real person with arms and legs and elbows. She knew from the pregnancy blogs online that the baby should have hardened bones now. So why did all its kicks feel so squirmy? Maybe there really was something wrong.

She settled on the steps of the front porch and searched on the internet, using many different variations on "baby kicks feeling wrong," or "quickening and bone density," before finally opening a new browser window and, with a resigned sigh, typing in "hearing voices during pregnancy" and "hallucinations AND pregnancy."

Thankfully, the rhododendrons nearby did not offer any commentary on her research. They just stirred in the gentle breeze every so often, like good rhododendrons should.

"If you know what's good for you, you'll stay quiet," Ashleigh muttered to herself as she stabbed her fingers violently at her laptop's keyboard. "I've got a pair of hedge clippers in the shed and ample free time on my hands."

The sun got lower and lower as she worked, her efforts only stopping when Kyle's car pulled into their driveway.

Ashleigh jumped up and closed the laptop with a snap. She ran over to Kyle as he got out of the car and hugged him tightly around the neck. He hugged her back and stroked her hair, murmuring "Everything ok, baby?"

She buried her face in his neck for a moment, breathing in his familiar smell. Finally, she nodded into his neck and pulled back to look at his face. She had initially thought to tell him about the terrifying events of that afternoon, but as she looked into his calm brown eyes, so serene and full of concern, she found that she couldn't do it. The words that were trying to bubble forth from her lips would surely land her in a psych ward somewhere. What would THAT mean for their baby?

She pasted on a smile and kissed her husband. "I'm fine. Just got a little distracted today…. uh…looking at baby names. I didn't notice the time. Dinner isn't ready. I'm sorry, baby."

Kyle laughed and stroked her cheek. "You have every right to get distracted. And dinner isn't only your responsibility, you know. I admit I'm not the best cook in this house, but I bet I can whip up a tofu scramble or something for us. Why don't you go relax on the couch while I cook, and I'll make you a cup of tea? You can read me your favorite baby names while I work."

* * *

Ten minutes later Ashleigh was tucked into the couch with her laptop and a cup of peppermint tea. The throw pillows that had been so conspiratorial earlier had been separated: one was behind her back and one under her laptop to protect her legs from the warmth of the computer. She was proud of herself that she managed to sound so normal, calling out name suggestions to Kyle while warily watching every loose object in room for any sign of life.

Thankfully, Kyle's dinner didn't take very long to make, and Ashleigh was soon able to escape to the kitchen table to eat. She found that in spite of—or perhaps because of—all the stress of the afternoon, she was ravenously hungry. She devoured several portions of dinner and even the bite or two Kyle left on his plate as they carried their dishes over to the sink. She thanked him for dinner and assented when he offered to do the dishes, leaning against the countertop and chatting idly with him about his day at work. It was so normal, so peaceful. Perhaps all she had needed was some real food; maybe it was just a low blood sugar thing that had happened to her.... could low blood sugar cause hallucinations? She made a mental note to check on that later, once her nearly dead laptop had recharged.

* * *

Over the next several weeks Ashleigh found that her appetite had returned with renewed force. She began eating several times a day and found that now she could not get enough meat. Their grocery bill doubled as Ashleigh began buying chicken, beef and pork in large quantities and cooking as if for an army each evening. One week, ground beef went on sale AND she had a coupon, so she was able to afford several pounds of it. Ashleigh became so hungry driving home that she reached into the bag on the passenger seat, poked a hole in the cellophane wrap, and picked out little nibbles of the raw meat for a snack on the drive. The little Christmas tree-shaped air freshener hanging on Ashleigh's rear-view-mirror made a few disparaging "tsk" sounds, but she flicked it with her finger, and it hushed right up.

She had just finished making a huge shepherd's pie for dinner when the phone rang. Kyle was working late; he had told her so this morning. She picked up her phone and peered at the screen. It was from a number she didn't recognize. "Hello?"

"Collect call from Hunter Phillips. Do you accept the charges?"

Ashleigh sighed in exasperation. "Yes...." There was a click as she was connected. "Hunter? What the hell?!"

"Sorry, sis. I got picked up last night...I only had a few beers, I swear, but there was this sobriety checkpoint and the cop whipped out the breathalyzer and I swear I didn't get to see the reading, but he said I was over the limit and cuffed me right then and there. So, can you come bail me out? Also, they, uh, towed my car so we'll also need to go pick it up from the impound lot."

Ashleigh took the phone away from her ear and stared at it for a moment. Then she put it back up to her head and said very calmly "No."

"No? Wait, what? No...you won't bail me out?"

"No, Hunter, I will not. I think you should call Mom. I'm very busy at the moment and I am tired of bailing your sorry ass out all the time. Maybe she can help you for a change because I'm not going to." He started to protest, but Ashleigh resolutely pushed the button to end the call, then tossed her phone onto the counter. She dug out a serving spoon from the drawer and began to eat the shepherd's pie straight out of the casserole dish.

There was a loud cheer from all around her. The potholder told her **I'M SO PROUD OF YOU. THAT'S OUR GIRL,** while the soap pump jiggled its nozzle at her in an approving nod. The angel figurine could be heard clapping from the other room, and even the oven was now smiling at her.

Ashleigh couldn't help herself and giggled at the attention. She took a bow to each of her fans in turn, then returned to shoveling the food into her mouth.

They all talked amongst themselves for a while as she ate, mostly discussing Hunter's many shortcomings. The conversation took a strange turn as the toaster made the quiet suggestion that... perhaps.... something should be done about him. There was a general murmur of agreement at this, and then the knives in the knife block started arguing with the drain cleaner under the sink about which would be the best way to get Hunter out of everyone's hair permanently.

The food in Ashleigh's mouth suddenly tasted as dry as sawdust. It took huge effort, but eventually she swallowed the bite and said "P-permanently? Are you saying someone should kill him? Th-that's terrible. He's my brother, you guys. Why would I kill him?"

Something nudged her arm, and Ashleigh looked down to see the soap pump looking at her earnestly. She patted it, and even pumped out a quick squirt to eat for old times' sake. The soap pump hopped closer. She leaned down to look at it on its level, eye to eye. It spoke to her slowly and clearly.

HE WOULD BE A TERRIBLE INFLUENCE ON THE BABY. DO YOU REALLY WANT THAT?

"N-no, I guess I don't." The pump bent down and nudged her spoon with its nozzle as if to say "Eat up. You're going to need it." She took up her spoon again and ate a few more large bites. Then she called the police station back and told them she would be there in a while to bail Hunter out. The baby was squirming madly inside her, and although her skin was feeling stretched and her body heavy and tired, still she ate more and more, as if her body contained a bottomless pit dug out by the frenetic motions of her little passenger.

* * *

Kyle was tired. It had been a long day at work with the software upgrades being pushed out. Ashleigh had told him that morning she had planned to make a huge dinner, so he was really looking forward to cracking a beer and having a huge portion of whatever she had made. He hadn't called Ashleigh to say he was on the way home since he was even later than he had hoped; she needed her rest now more than ever, and she was hopefully sleeping soundly upstairs. It was now only a few hours until dawn.

He pulled into the driveway. That's odd, he thought. Why are all the lights on? And why is Hunter's car here? He went to the front door and turned the handle. It was unlocked. His heart started to pound. He opened the door and was met by a horrifying sight.

There was blood everywhere: all over the couch, spattered on the walls, and Hunter's body was sprawled at an odd angle across the sofa's throw pillows. It looked like someone had taken almost every knife out of the block in the kitchen and driven them one after another into his stomach and chest. Blood was pooled under him, soaking into the plaid cushions. Kyle finally found his voice and called out "Ashleigh????" His mind raced, wondering if there had been some sort of home invasion. He was terrified that he might find his wife in the same state as Hunter somewhere else in the house, so he called out to her, praying that she would answer. She did.

"I'm in heeeeeere!" She sang the word out strangely. She was in the kitchen, but he didn't see her at first since she was sitting on the floor, hidden behind the kitchen island. Kyle fell to his knees in front of her, his shoes slipping in the blood smeared all over the tile.

Ashleigh was leaning up against the oven door, sitting in a puddle of blood. There was something in her hands. It looked almost like an octopus: long, boneless protrusions dangled and smacked wetly against her arms as she held it. Blood was smeared all around her mouth, and she bent to take another bite out of the thing in her hands. Kyle gestured wordlessly at her, unable to ask what was happening. Ashleigh chewed her bite, swallowed, and waved the thing at him as if in greeting. Droplets of blood hit him in the face as she spoke.

"Linda was wrong; I should have known it all along. You really can't trust those pyramid scheme people, Kyle. They're just out to make a buck, they really don't care about helping anyone. Linda kept feeding me all these pills and essential oils and stuff and <u>I trusted her</u>." She tore another bite off with her teeth here and shook her head sadly. "But it wasn't a baby, Kyle. I mean, maybe at first it was a baby, but then this thing ate it. So I'm eating it right back." She laughed, her mouth open wide and stained red, her head sagging back against the oven for a moment, the monstrosity in her hand dangling its tendrils into her lap.

"Ashleigh...what happened to Hunter?" Kyle had found his voice, but it only reached a whisper.

Ashleigh narrowed her eyes and leaned in toward him. She reached out and tapped him on the nose with one red-stained finger. "He had to go," she told Kyle solemnly. "He would have been a bad influence on the baby. He fought me pretty hard, though. I knew I should have listened to the Drano's advice and just put rat poison in his soup or something...but then he fought back and I...I just lost my temper, I guess. I don't really remember how he ended up with all those knives in him like that. But I kept one for myself so I could do my very own home birth. Ha ha...like we always wanted, remember? Except instead of pushing the baby out, Kyle, I had to pull it. I had to cut myself open, and I pulled and pulled. It didn't want to come out, Kyle, but I won in the end. I think it did something to me on the way out, though. I can't really feel my legs anymore, which is why I'm just going to stay here next to my new friend, the oven." She patted the blood-smeared glass door behind her. "I've named him Ken, short for Kenmore, and he says he'll just prop me up until I'm done eating. Oh! Hey! I've been so rude, sitting here chattering away while you just got home from work. I bet you're starving, Kyle...d'you want a bite?" She held out the monster, the parasite, that had been living inside her. It wriggled at him weakly, as if reaching out to be held. Kyle was still frozen in shock and dismay, so Ashleigh shrugged and took another squelching bite. "Hey Kyle, I'm getting kind of tired, but I don't want to leave my buddy Ken here. Do you think you could grab a blanket for me? And maybe a few Band Aids? But make sure not to listen to the first aid kit…. it's a damned liar." Ashleigh was blinking slowly at him now, her eyes heavy-lidded.

Kyle finally moved, backing away from his wife, pulling out his cell phone to dial 911. Ashleigh held up her parasite once more and said "You really should try it, Kyle. Remember our first date? Calamari? It's almost like that, except really gross." She laughed weakly at the joke, as Kyle staggered to the front door to wait for the ambulance and the police cars, and to throw up in the bushes outside.

RYE HUMOR

Benny heard his head pound even before he came fully-awake that morning. The light was way too bright; it stabbed at his eyelids. His mouth tasted like something had died there. *Here we go again*, he thought, and gingerly rolled to his side, away from the window's painful glow.

He opened his eyes, finally. Everything was a bit blurry, and he had to throw up. He groaned as he rolled clumsily off the bed and staggered into the bathroom. After he finished and rinsed out his mouth, he reached under the bathroom sink for a bottle of Gatorade. He always kept some handy these days. He opened the cap and chugged down the yellowish liquid in time with the throbbing in his temples. He started the shower on full blast to hot; the steam would be good for him.

He tossed the empty Gatorade bottle into the wastebasket across the room and stepped into the shower, letting the hot water beat on his face. The headache was easing already, but he had a few more tricks up his sleeve for the full cure.

Benny dressed for work and went downstairs, where he cracked a beer and made himself a huge bacon and egg sandwich. The combined greasy breakfast and hair of the dog helped immensely. Benny managed to get out the door almost on time and climbed up into his landscaping truck to head to his first job of the day. He got steady work as a landscaper here in Snowbridge, as it seemed that almost nobody in the community liked to mow their own grass or mulch their own yard.

That wouldn't have been enough to live on if it wasn't for his biggest client: the HOA. They had driven a hard bargain with him...he had joked to Lili as he signed that the ink in his signature may as well have been his own blood. But, so long as he kept exactly to the terms and deadlines stipulated in his contract, they paid him well and promptly. Benny kept to a strict rotating schedule of mowing the common areas, planting seasonally appropriate flowers near the entrance signs and around the dog park, and pruning the trees lining the main roads into the development.

All things considered, he made a good living...good enough to buy his own house in a nice place like Snowbridge. He liked to work outside, even in the heat and cold, he liked the contemplative solitude of mowing yards and planting flowers, and he liked that he only had to work during the day. It was a much better schedule than he used to have as a bartender. There, the hours were long, especially on closing shift, and he had to be mostly amiable to everyone. Of course, it was easy to sneak a nip here and there without management noticing, which made for a nice job perk as well. But here he didn't have a boss looking over his shoulder and only rarely had to get help from Brian, a local teen in the neighborhood, on big jobs, so he could easily fill his hydration bottle with whatever liquid courage he needed during the day, and nobody was the wiser.

For example, today his "iced tea" was about equal parts cheap rye whiskey and water, with some ice thrown in for good measure. Today wouldn't be terribly hot, but it would be sunny. He took a sip and felt the whiskey burn its way down his throat. He settled his headphones securely over his ears, cued up his Lynyrd Skynyrd-heavy playlist, started the tractor, and began his workday.

Benny found mowing to be a soothing activity. He enjoyed creating lines of clean-cut grass on the diagonal, watching the little field mice and snakes scurry out of his path, with the smell of grass and clover thick in his nose. There were times that he finished a job and honestly couldn't have said how long he'd been working. He would reach an almost meditative state, where ideas came and went in a swirl of color and formlessness.

He was just reaching the zone when his tractor suddenly came upon a fox laying in the grass. It didn't jump up out of his way like animals normally did. Benny cut the engine and climbed down out of the seat. Foxes were normally nocturnal, and this little guy should have been back in his den by now. He walked slowly up to it, trying to seem as nonthreatening as possible. Once he got close and managed to get a good look, he could see that the fox had a compound fracture on its hind leg. "Aw, poor little guy," Benny murmured to it as he crouched next to the injured animal. He reached a tentative hand out to it. The fox's eyes were bright, its nose twitching like crazy. Thinking the better of grabbing a feral injured animal with his bare hands, Benny quickly took off his flannel shirt, leaving his sweaty undershirt on underneath. He gently scooped the fox up in the shirt, wrapping it carefully like baby while cradling its injured leg. Other than making a characteristic scream once, likely due to an unintentional jostle of bone-on-bone, it stayed relatively still and silent.

Taking the keys to the mower with him, he abandoned the lawn half-done and loped back to his truck with the fox in his arms. He tucked the animal in on the passenger seat and drove carefully to the wildlife rescue in town, keeping his hand gently on the trembling fox's back for comfort.

He carried the fox into the lobby and explained the situation to the workers there. "I just couldn't leave him, you know? And sometimes if you call animal control, they just put them out of their misery, and I couldn't have that on my conscience; it would feel like I called a hit on him or something. Please, promise me that you'll take care of him. He seems scared to death. He's barely made a noise at all." The people at the animal rescue were understanding and smiled at him, thanking him for his kindness and promising to nurse the fox back to health. They asked him to place the fox in a dog crate in the examination room while they gathered up what supplies were needed. Benny bent to put him in, saying a quick goodbye. But as he drew his hands away, the fox made a sharp movement with its head and bit his hand, hard and deep, in the space between his thumb and first finger. Blood welled up on his palm and the back of his hand, dripping on the floor. "OW!" He yelled, jumping back from the cage door and scrambling to the sink to rinse the wound. He wadded up paper towels from the dispenser to staunch the bleeding.

The noise had attracted a few of the workers, and they now crowded around him. An older lady, her greying hair pulled into a bun and exuding authority, shook her head and made a "tsk" sound. "You'll want to go to the hospital, I'm afraid, sir. That looks pretty deep. You likely need stitches, and probably a series of rabies shots. That's just bad luck, considering you made it the whole way here unscathed."

The paper towel was soaking through now. Benny gritted his teeth and applied even more pressure. The staff jumped into action and quickly packed and wrapped his hand using the vet supplies around them. One of them, a young woman with rectangular green glasses, offered to drive him to the hospital, but he waved her off. "Nah. I'm left-handed. It's fine. I can drive myself. That way you all can focus on fixing up that little shit that bit me." He smiled and laughed ruefully. The gathered staff members patted his shoulder and walked him out. The one who had offered him a ride even opened his car door and helped him buckle the seat belt before waving him out the driveway. *Maybe I should go back there sometime; she's kind of cute,* Benny thought as he maneuvered the car back onto the road, chancing one more look at the woman in the rearview mirror.

At the hospital, he waited for 90 minutes in the ER to be seen for triage. Apparently, arriving with professional-looking bandages in place made the staff assume you weren't really bleeding *that* much and could afford to wait while they took little Timmy with a sore throat back to be seen first. His hand was throbbing badly by then, and Benny was glad that he had finished the last of his "tea" in his car before going into the ER itself. The whiskey certainly had taken the edge off. He couldn't imagine how he would be feeling right now without it.

"Benjamin MacKenzie?" The nurse called out in a bored sort of way from the swinging door at the end of the waiting room. *Finally.* Benny got up and hurried over to her.

"That's me!" He tried to smile at her, but at this point, after all the hubbub of the afternoon and now the long wait while in pain, it was basically a grimace. He needn't have even tried. The nurse didn't react at all, and simply turned and walked back down the hall, gesturing vaguely over her shoulder that he should go into a room off the hall with a number "2" nailed to it. Benny went in and sat in the plastic chair waiting for him.

The nurse plopped herself onto the rolling stool at the desk in front of the laptop. She proceeded to force him to get weighed, have his temperature taken, and even have his blood pressure checked without asking him once what sort of ailment he had. He was very glad she decided to use his left arm for blood pressure, as the squeezing of the cuff would likely have made his hand hurt worse.

Finally, she asked him "So, what brings you in here today?" In reply, he simply held up his bandaged hand. "It looks like you've already been seen by someone," she said to him flatly, a hint of impatience in her voice.

"I was bitten by a fox that I brought into the wildlife rescue for treatment. He had a broken leg. After he bit me, the vet there put this on me and said I would need stitches and a rabies shot. I have to say, I'm not looking forward to either. Do they still give you that one in your butt?"

"Why don't you let an actual doctor decide what the proper treatment is, and not the vet, hm?" She typed some things into his chart, clicked the mouse a few times, then stood up from the stool with a sigh. "Follow me, please." She opened a door on the opposite wall from which they had entered and escorted him to a hospital bed with curtains hanging around it in a large room full of identical beds and identical curtains. Benny threw himself onto the bed and waited another 15 minutes for the doctor to come. He was obviously very much in a hurry when he finally arrived. He proceeded to quickly unwrap Benny's wound, grimace, and bark out a few commands to the nurse standing by. After a flurry of activity and a numbing shot to Benny's wrist, the doctor stitched up the bites on both sides of Benny's hand with lightning speed. As he finished the last knot, he looked up into Benny's face and said "You were right, you know. You do need a rabies shot. But don't worry, it only goes in your arm." Benny laughed out loud in relief.

The doctor froze a moment as Benny's breath passed his nostrils. *Oops...the whiskey*, Benny thought. The doctor straightened up and crossed his arms, looking Benny up and down in a judgmental fashion.

"Did you decide to self-medicate just today, sir? Or is this a common thing?"

Benny shrugged and held his hands wide. "Aw, come on doc. Cut me some slack. That little bugger's teeth were sharp. And I was waiting quite a while to get seen here, you know."

The doctor made a noncommittal noise in his throat and looked at Benny's chart again. "And how many drinks would you say you have in a week, Mr. Mackenzie?" He typed something into the laptop, then looked at Benny expectantly.

"A week? Uh... oh, I don't know. I mean, I work outside all day. Who doesn't like a beer when they come in after yard work?"

"So.... seven? Or do you have more than one beer after yard work?" There was an awkward pause. Benny didn't know what to say and simply shrugged. "Ah...well, sir. I have to tell you, I can't in good conscience prescribe you any narcotics considering you already seem to have a substance abuse problem." He looked smug now, his earlier professionalism had evaporated.

"Hey hey hey! I don't have a problem! You can't get an idea of my life from the 5 minutes you've talked to me here. This was a very weird day for me, you know?" Benny was standing now, facing off with the doctor.

"There's no reason to get hostile, sir. My nurse here is going to give you your rabies shot, and you can be on your way. Try not to take any Tylenol for the pain, ok? It's for your own good; your liver is working hard enough as it is. You will also need to schedule a few follow-up appointments to get the stitches out and for your other rabies shots. It's a series of four, usually." The doctor had taken off his gloves and was now throwing them away, turning his back on Benny. He threw the next comment over his shoulder. "You should consider joining AA. I've seen far too many people like you in my career, so I don't believe for a second that you aren't an alcoholic. Have a good day." With that, he swept past the curtains, leaving his nurse standing awkwardly with a syringe in her hand. She looked almost scared.

Benny held up his hands in a calming gesture and sat down again, sighing and rolling up the sleeve of his t-shirt so she could do the shot. She handed him his discharge paperwork, directed him to the check-out window, and fairly flew out of the curtained area and out of sight.

Benny checked out, made the appointments he was supposed to, and walked out of the ER to his truck. He still had to finish at least the common area mowing. There would be hell to pay from the HOA if he didn't fulfill his contract to the letter. The other job he had planned for today he could catch up on tomorrow. That one was a new lawn mowing customer he hadn't even met yet...only texted with. He would apologize to them tomorrow in person.

It was not easy driving with his hand now, since it was still numb from when the doctor put in the stitches. He drove back to Snowbridge, past all the signs on the main street saying "If you lived here you'd be home by now" and "Dog Park! Playground! Pool! Daycare Center!" and "Build to Suit, SF Homes from the Lower $200's."

Benny parked near the common area again and dug into his duffel bag in the backseat for his emergency flask. *Just a little bit left to go, man*, he told himself. *We can do this.* He took a swig of moonshine and felt it burn down to his stomach, a little fortification for the rest of the job. Finishing mowing the grass took longer that it normally would have, as he was now working one-handed, but luckily, he had a huge zero-turn machine that did most of the work for him. No other animals appeared to make trouble for him, and so he pulled the mower up onto the truck's trailer, hooked it back up to his truck, and drove the short distance home. Cutting the engine, Benny laid his head on the steering wheel a minute, his head pounding. He needed to eat. With all the hubbub of the day's events, he'd forgotten. With a groan, Benny hauled himself out of the car and went inside. He made himself a frozen pizza, ate the whole thing washed down with a six-pack of beer, then took a large glass of whiskey with him to bed for a much-needed night's sleep.

The next morning's hangover wasn't too bad, all things considered. But perhaps it just seemed easier in comparison to his hand, which was throbbing like someone was beating it with a hammer. *Damn that fox*, Benny thought as he wrapped his hand in a grocery bag in order to take a shower and not soak through the dressing. He had breakfast (cereal and a Bloody Maria), packed himself a lunch, and locked up his house to go to work. He'd start with the job left over from yesterday. Benny checked his phone for the text from the lady who wanted him to mow and was glad to see it was just the next street over. He pulled the truck up in front of the client's house. It was one of the smaller single-family house models sold in Snowbridge, built in the mirror image to his own, but Benny could see that they had added the front porch and the sunroom. He knocked on the door, and when it opened, he was surprised to see the pretty woman with the green glasses from the animal rescue the day before.

"Oh! Hi!" Benny was annoyed at how weird and high his voice sounded to his own ears. "Remember me?" He held up his bandaged hand and tried to grin charmingly.

"Oh, hi! You're feeling ok now, then?" She asked him rather cautiously, closing the door slightly.

"Yeah, sure am. They fixed me right up. But that's not why I'm here. I swear I didn't stalk you or anything. I'm your lawn guy." He gestured over his shoulder back at the truck with his good thumb. "I got a little delayed yesterday at the ER and didn't make it out here to work. I wanted to apologize for being a day late and let you know I was on the job today."

The relief shone on her face and his newest client opened her door a bit wider again. "Oh! That's so funny! Small world. Are you sure you'll be ok to mow, though?"

"No problem! I'm an all-around professional, you know. I don't just rescue wildlife." Benny winked at her at this and was gratified to see her not only smile but give a little giggle. She was really a nice-looking woman.

"Um, ok. I'll let you get to it, then? I have to leave for work...but I really am glad you're feeling better. The fox was doing fine last night after we set his leg. The vet says it will be just a few weeks and he'll be good as new." She was now gathering her purse, her water bottle, and a packed lunch from the hall table. She came out onto the porch and locked the door, then held out her hand to him. "See you later.... uh...Benny, was it?" Benny reached out to shake her hand, then realized she would have to shake his bandaged one. They both shared a laugh, and there was a pause while she rearranged everything so she could shake his left hand instead. "I'm Sherry. Nice to meet you again, under better circumstances. Thanks for the help with mowing.... I'll, uh, see you later, I guess?" She smiled down at him. Her eyes crinkled at the corners when she smiled. Her green-rimmed glasses made her eyes seem even bigger. Benny smiled back, his chest warming like he'd just taken a shot of moonshine.

He watched her drive away, then shook himself and got to work on Sherry's lawn. Instead of listening to his music, he pictured her face and those eyes looking at him and smiling. Her face was even better food for mediation than Lynyrd Skynyrd.

* * *

Over the next few weeks, Benny though of Sherry often. He tried to catch her at home when he came to mow the yard but was unlucky. In due time, his stitches came out and he continued his rabies shot series. The nurse at his final appointment, who had apparently read the doctor's notes, handed him a pamphlet for the Alcoholics Anonymous chapter that met each week at the local library. He gave her a curt nod and shoved the paper into his pocket, stalking out the door. *Busybodies,* Benny thought. *They don't know...they just think they know everything, don't they? They didn't have to see what happened... the look on her face, the way she screamed as she died...* It had taken a lot of whiskey to make that memory go quiet. It was better this way. Why didn't they mind their own damn business?

The dark thoughts followed him home, where the flashbacks started.

Benny hadn't been a whiskey man back then, but he'd liked to smoke. One night he and his buddy had a little fun seeing what patterns they could make with lit cigarettes on bare skin. The girl hadn't been into the game, so they'd tied her down. Then the friend reminded Benny there was a knife in his pocket. The knife made even better patterns, and his friend had had lots of suggestions for how to make them. He'd taken over, then, and things had gotten ugly.

He upended the moonshine bottle and gulped again and again, his eyes burning and tears streaming down his cheeks as the drink scorched its way into his stomach, burning away the memories and the sound of her blood choking her at the end. Benny fell asleep in his chair that night, the empty bottle dropping to the carpet next to him. His last drunken thought as he passed out was of Sherry's smile.

* * *

The next morning was not kind. Benny crawled, literally crawled, into the bathroom and lay on the cool tile floor for a few long minutes. His head felt like it was going to explode, and even the thought of trying to stand up was nauseating. He pulled himself up to a beastly crouch at the sink and drank cupped handfuls of water. Luckily, the medicine cabinet in the bathroom had a whole bottle of aspirin in it. He took four, helped along by more handfuls of tap water. Then he sank to the floor again, resting his back against the sink cabinet and staring blearily up at the ceiling. He used all the willpower he had to keep the aspirin down long enough to do him some good, and all told, he spent a good hour in the bathroom practicing very hard the art of "not moving at all."

When the floor stopped spinning long enough, he staggered into the kitchen. I'll start with crackers, Benny thought, then if I feel up to it, I'll try for eggs or something. The aspirin was just starting to work, so he didn't want to exacerbate the headache by throwing up.

While he chewed, Benny leaned against the refrigerator, its surface cool against his aching head. I can't keep doing this, he thought. Maybe he was wrong...maybe he really could make it without the booze. God, he'd love to get up just one morning without feeling like shit. Benny reached into his pocket and pulled out the AA pamphlet. Maybe they could help. Lots of people swore by AA, but was he beyond their kind of help? He sighed. It might be worth a try. If he could stop feeling like this, maybe he would be the kind of guy a girl like Sherry would want to spend time with. Maybe he could stop being so lonely. Maybe...

Benny stood up straight for the first time that morning. Maybe with help, it could work. He could be worth something more than being a lawn guy for the cursed HOA. Maybe he could be interesting.... attractive to someone. *Someone like Sherry?* The voice in his head whispered, then winked. *Yeah...someone like her,* he answered it sullenly.

He walked to the stove to make breakfast. It was going to be a busy day.

* * *

Benny mowed and planted and mulched all day. With no hair of the dog in his system to help, the headache remained, but he pushed past it. He was actually ahead of schedule on his jobs for a change. He mowed the Greene's yard and planted some annuals in the front for them near the rhododendrons. Ashleigh looked a bit heavier than when he last saw her...was she pregnant? Then he took a quick trip home to shower and put on a clean shirt before driving to the library for the AA meeting.

When he got to the meeting room there were already a half-dozen people present. A few were getting coffee from the table at the back, chatting amongst themselves. They seemed to understand that Benny didn't want to talk just yet, and they gave him space as he poured himself a coffee and stood against the wall to wait.

Someone had posted a sign with the 12 steps on it. He wandered over to read them. After reading the last one, Benny shrugged inwardly. There were a lot of references to God, which nagged at Benny's lapsed Catholic upbringing, but he had come this far with an open mind, and he should keep it that way for a while, at least. For Sherry's sake, and for his own.

The meeting was called to order and Benny sat near the back of the room. He was relieved that nobody pushed him to talk or share, although "new faces" were welcomed at the beginning of the meeting itself. If he'd been pushed into public speaking right off the bat, that might have been the end of Benny's experiment right there. He listened as other people shared their stories of drinking, of blackouts, of hiding their habits from their families and coworkers, and of their coping strategies for the mornings that were all too familiar. A tiny flame of hope began to grow in his mind. Maybe he *could* do this. Maybe he could pull himself out of this cycle. Maybe...

That night Benny went home and drank orange juice—straight orange juice—with his dinner. It tasted odd and almost too sweet without any vodka, but it wasn't that bad either. He watched a rerun of "Cheers" until his eyes felt sleepy, and then he brushed his teeth and went to bed like a normal person. It felt weird, but in a good way

Going to sleep on purpose instead of drinking until passing out was a different experience, and it took much longer. He dreamed colorfully, chaotically, and incomprehensibly until 6 in the morning, when he woke suddenly and completely. The sun was streaming through the curtains, and Benny was surprised to realize that he was shaking uncontrollably. He felt awful, like he had the flu. He was nauseated (almost like his normal morning stomach, but not quite), and his heart was pounding like he'd just run a marathon.

Benny reached for his phone on the nightstand and googled his symptoms. The fourth result caught his eye: a Wikipedia article on Alcohol withdrawal syndrome.

"Well, fuck," Benny said out loud, and read the article from his bed, squinting in the low light of the phone. *It's almost not even worth it to quit, is it?* the voice murmured in his ear.

Benny waved his hand in the air as if shooing away a bee. "Shut up, you. I'm not listening. It says here that auditory and even visual hallucinations are common. You are a figment of my imagination."

Oh, I am, am I? Just a figment, huh? That's cute. And I suppose it was just a figment that hurt that girl? Or

was it you? Are you, you...? Or are you, me? If I'm just a figment, then you're the only one here...and that means it was your fault. Are you ready to face that idea without good old Johnnie Walker? I don't think so; you haven't the strength. Look at what you've become, trying to get rid of me. The whiskey may have turned my volume down a little, but I'm still here, you know. I just got bored. I've had so much free time on my hands...well...your hands....to think of all sorts of new games we can play with the next one. You know there will be a next one, don't you, Benny-my-boy?

Benny plugged his headphones into his phone and turned up his playlist as loud as his eardrums could stand, which seemed to drown out the voice. Then he went downstairs to try and eat something.

As he stirred the oatmeal on the stove, he thought back to the 12 steps. *Number one, admit there's a problem.* He nodded to himself. Hell, yeah. He had a problem. *Number two, put faith in a power greater than oneself to restore sanity.* Now, Benny knew well and good that there were several powers greater than himself, and that one of them was currently being drowned out by "Gimme Three Steps" by good old Lynyrd. He would love to be restored to sanity, as the lyrics went. But so long as that voice was around... he shook his head to clear it. What was next, again? Oh, right. *Number three, turn one's will and lives over to God.* Benny made a grunting sound deep in his throat. If God was so great and could fix everything for him, why hadn't He done it already? Wouldn't that have been faster, and a lot less trouble for everyone involved?

Benny dumped his oatmeal into a bowl and sprinkled it liberally with brown sugar. The playlist switched over to "Sweet Home Alabama," which was a nice change of tone. Benny finished his breakfast in a slightly better mood and set about getting ready to go to work for the day. It was noticeably faster without being hung over, his pounding head and shakes notwithstanding.

Work felt like it took more effort than usual, but Benny kept his headphones at full blast and put his whole mind to each job, from trimming down the hedges surrounding the dog park to mowing the common area near the playground. It was a weekday, and school was in session, so it was relatively calm in the neighborhood. He looked at his phone schedule to see what the afternoon's job was.

The appointment reminder jumped out at him, and his heart skipped a beat. "Sherry — Mowing." She hadn't been around the last several times he'd been there to work, and he was disappointed that he hadn't had the excuse of dropping off an invoice to try and see her. He was paid promptly via Venmo the evening after each mowing job.

Is she avoiding you? I wonder why.... The whisper came through clearly despite the blaring music.

Benny grunted and started up his truck to drive to Sherry's. It was better not to answer the voice; he would just provoke it. He pulled up alongside her house, backed the mower off the ramp, and started his diagonal pattern on the grass. As he passed near to the front door, a movement caught his eye. Sherry was standing on the porch watching him. When she saw him make eye contact, she smiled at him tentatively and waved. She looked nice today: her hair was in a ponytail, and she was wearing yoga pants and a t-shirt. Benny killed the engine, got off of the seat and walked over, removing his headphones. "Hey there," he said. "Haven't seen you in a while. How's things?"

Sherry shrugged her shoulders, her ponytail swinging. "Yeah...it's been pretty busy at work. I haven't been able to get a lot of errands done, so I took a half day off today."

"Any update on the fox?"

"The fox is good. We'll release him this week, I think. He seems pretty much back to his old foxy self." Sherry smiled at him and tilted her head. The effect was adorable. "So...I have a huge favor to ask you. I'm sorry I didn't text to ask you before now, but I bought some annuals for the flowerbeds out back that I'd love to have planted. Would you possibly have some time after mowing today?" Her sheepish smile made a warm wave spread out from his chest.

He couldn't help himself. He grinned back at her hugely, like an idiot. He walked a few steps toward her and shook his finger at her in mock reproach. "Well, I suppose I can, but don't let it get out to the rest of the neighborhood, you hear? Then everyone will want me to be all flexible, and I just can't have that." He was close enough to her now that he could have touched the tip of her upturned nose with his finger, but he didn't.

Sherry giggled and nodded at him. "It's a deal. Thank you so much. Just let me know how much I owe you for the extra work." She turned to go back inside.

"Uh, wait. Sherry? Can I ask you something?"

She turned back to him, a slight smile on her face. His heart skipped a beat again.

"I...uh.... this is going to sound so awkward and creepy, and I don't mean it to.... but...are you seeing anyone?" He paused, reeling at his own utter lack of eloquence. "It's just that...I was wondering if you'd like to have a bee—uh, I mean, a coffee sometime? I mean....do you drink coffee? I don't, myself. I'm more of a hot cocoa guy, but to each their own." He was completely floundering now, and if she was looking for a manly type, he was sure he'd just blown it with the whole "hot cocoa" admission.

Sherry was standing perfectly still, staring at him. Benny was sure she was about to run inside and lock the door, but she surprised him by giving him an appraising sort of look and saying. "Hm.... I might be open to that. But you have to answer me a question first, and it's very important." She took a few steps toward him on the porch, leaning down at the steps and looking him dead in the eye. He could smell her shampoo. It was like coconuts and sunshine. His breath caught.

"Marshmallows or whipped cream?" Her eyes twinkled at him behind the glasses.

Benny let out his breath in a loud burst of laughter. "Ah! Well.... the way I see it, why not both?" He held his hands out to his sides in a wide shrug. Sherry laughed too.

"All right then. You passed the test; it's a date. Are you busy this evening? Around 6?"

"6 is perfect." Benny said. "Would you like me to pick you up or do you prefer to meet me at the Cafe?"

"I'll meet you. I'm looking forward it. See you, Benny." Sherry turned and walked to her front door again, this time resolutely closing it behind her.

The warmth in Benny's chest felt hotter now. *She said yes. Even though I was an idiot, she said yes. Oh, yes.* He grinned to himself and walked back to the mower. In fact, he grinned pretty much steadily the rest of the day until he pulled into a parking spot at the Hydeout Cafe at exactly 5:55 that evening.

She was waiting for him at a table in the corner. Two cups were already in front of her, the whipped cream and sprinkles towering several inches above their rims. She stood up when he came in, smiling at him and waving.

"Hey! Sorry, I was trying to get here in time to wait for you, not the other way around." Benny came over to her and paused a space away, feeling glad enough to see her that he'd love to hug her, but knowing that that was not the right move. After a short awkward pause, he held out his hand. She placed her hand in his and squeezed a moment. Hers was warm, and soft. He let her go and pulled out the chair opposite her to sit. "Is one of these science experiments meant for me? Funny, I thought we were having cocoa." Sherry laughed softly.

"Eh, we are. I'm sure there's some under that whipped cream somewhere." She scooped some of the topping up in her spoon and ate it, winking at him.

They sat in the Cafe for over an hour, ordering a second cocoa each. They talked about all sorts of things, from movies to books to music. Benny shared his Spotify playlist with her so she could hear more classic rock, and she promised to lend him some of her vinyl records of Ella Fitzgerald and Miles Davis. According to Sherry, it was the only real way to hear the greats.

Benny would have loved to continue the date. He was having the most wonderful time and feeling so incredibly happy and normal and ... sober ... for the first time in a long time. But, the whispers in his ear were getting steadily worse. It was as if all the sugar he'd had was exacerbating the problem.

Jazz? JAZZ?! Benny my boy, I sure hope you get into this girl's pants soon. There is absolutely never a reason for anyone in their right mind to be that into jazz and not be a hundred years old. Hey, Benny! Are you listening to me, man? Did you see the way that blouse fits her? I swear, if she arched her back a little you could definitely see her— Benny stood up suddenly, interrupting Sherry mid-sentence.

"Well, Sherry, I hate to break this short. I am having the most amazing time. But I've got a...well...an appointment...to get to, and, uh..." Benny trailed off awkwardly. Nice job, idiot, he thought, it's our first date and I'm already telling her about AA. He was sure that sort of bombshell would nuke his chances for good.

"Sure. I had a good time too. Maybe we can talk again sometime? I mean, you already have my number." She winked and stirred the last of her cocoa.

"Definitely," he smiled down at her. "And next time, it's my treat, I insist. You were too quick this time. Thank you for the sugar rush." He touched her hand where it lay on the table, then turned and walked out the door of the cafe.

The whisper in his ear had become a shout by the time Benny got to the truck. *You ARE an idiot, you idiot! She was into you! You could have gotten way farther with her tonight, but instead you're going to a meeting like a goddamn pussy. That's what you are, you pussy! Instead of GETTING it, you've BECOME it. You're pathetic. Running off to a meeting to talk about your feelings, leaving a hot little piece like her just sitting by herself. You've missed your chance now, Benny boy. This is why you're just a lonely little man, spending all your time mowing lawns and going to meetings. This is why you need me; you never had any follow-through.*

Benny started the engine and hunched his shoulders against the tirade. When he didn't respond, the voice changed its tactics.

Heyyyy, Benny boy. You know I'm just kidding around with you, right? Who has ever been a better wingman to you than me, eh? I help you get chicks, I

*always have great advice...who loves you, baby? Hey....
you know what I think? I think, after your little touchy-
feely meeting, you should take a walk to her house. We
can see if she leaves the curtains open while she changes
tonight. You know how to get into the backyard, and you
know where her bedroom is since you guys have the same
house plan...I bet you'd like to get a look at the goods, eh?
You haven't seen a woman for so long that wasn't on a
dirty movie. I mean, do you even remember what they
look like in real life?*

"Shut UP!" He shouted out loud, finally. His voice
rang loudly in the closed space of the truck's cab. The
voice fell silent and stayed that way all though the AA
meeting. Benny didn't share, again, but nobody seemed
to mind. He drove home with the radio turned up loud,
just in case.

When he parked in the driveway of his house, he sat
there in the darkened car for a few minutes, gripping the
steering wheel tightly. He could almost feel the voice's
eyes on him, waiting.

Finally, he reached a decision. He got out of the car,
locked it, and stalked up the street in the opposite direction
of Sherry's house. He looped around cul-de-sac after cul-
de-sac, trying to walk off the boiling energy he seemed to
feel. As his thumping footsteps passed Will and Ellie's
house, he heard someone call out to him.

"Hey there, are you alright?" It took Benny a
moment to locate the sound. Finally, he realized it was
coming from the bed of the truck in the driveway. Two
people were sitting in it, looking at him curiously. After a
second, he realized that it was just Will and Ellie. Benny
took a few steps toward them.

"Yeah, just needed to think, I guess. Sorry if I
disturbed you guys with your...whatever you're doing."

What *were* they doing? Why were they sitting in the bed of a truck in the middle of the night?

Ellie smiled at him and pointed at the night sky above. "There's supposed to be a meteor shower tonight. We're waiting for it to start. Are you sure you're ok?" She peered at him, concern showing in her brown eyes.

"Yeah, I'm totally fine. I'll let you get back to your meteors. See you guys later." And with that, Benny strode off again. Behind him, Will put his arm around Ellie again and they lay down in the truck's bed, gazing back up at the sky.

After a while, Benny found himself out of sidewalk. He was in the portion of the neighborhood still under construction. Ignoring the "NO TRESPASSING" signs, he strode across the cleared land waiting for new basements to be dug out. He climbed the mound of dirt beyond and sat on a large rock, looking up at the sky. There were no meteors yet. He heard a rustling noise off to his side. An animal was skulking around nearby, sniffing at the ground. In the moonlight he could see an odd coloring on its leg. No...not coloring. It didn't have hair on that leg, like it had been shaved off. There was a long scar running down its length in the bare spot. *Holy shit, it's the same fox. What are the odds?*

The little creature kept sniffing around. Benny held very still as it came closer, and then there was a rushing sound in his ears, like the combination of a strong wind and someone yelling all at once.

* * *

Benny's hands were wet. He was looking up at the moon again, but it was in a different place than it had been a minute ago. *What had happened?* He looked down at his hands. They were covered with something dark. And red. The ground around him was littered with scraps of fur and shards of bone. There was a pile of entrails at his feet. *The fox. Oh, God. What the hell have I done?*

Benny scrambled to his feet and backed away, his breath coming in short gasps. Desperately, he wiped his hands on the grass and leaves around him trying to clean them off. Then, he turned and ran as fast as he could toward his house, cutting through yards and hopping the low paddock-style fences which were the only ones allowed by the HOA. *At least that's one good thing about them*, Benny thought ruefully as he ran, *they don't keep pets or kids in worth a damn, and they're a bitch to paint, but at least they were easily scalable when you were in a hurry.*

Benny came to his back door at last and groped for his hidden key in the flowerbed. He let himself inside, sprinting upstairs, and took a long, scalding hot shower. The water ran red for a long time. The voice was silent now, but he could hear it smiling, the bastard.

He started a load of laundry with double soap and on a full hot cycle. If they didn't get clean, he would have to throw them away. Or maybe he should shred them up with the next mulching job.

He wanted a drink very badly.

Instead, Benny poured himself a tall glass of water and climbed into bed. He turned off all the lights and stared at the ceiling. He had forgotten to close the curtains, and now he could see the occasional meteor streak through the sky. As his eyes started to close Benny heard the voice whisper to him, very quietly:

That was fun. I'm back, Benny-my-boy, and I'm here to stay.

* * *

Just after sunrise, the cellphone on Benny's nightstand buzzed twice in quick succession. He rolled over and tilted the phone so he could see the screen. There was a text from Sherry. He sat up all the way, reveling in the fact that his head didn't spin at the movement... another new and wondrous morning experience.

"Hey! So, I was thinking...can you cook? How about I come over for dinner sometime this week? I'll bring dessert." The text was followed by a winking emoji.

Benny's mouth went dry. He hadn't scared her off; she wanted to see him again. He quickly typed out his answer. "I'm no chef, but I make a mean chili. Are you ok with beef? Or do you prefer vegetarian?"

The reply was almost instantaneous. "Carnivore here. I'm in. :)"

They scheduled dinner for that very night and signed off. Benny got up with a spring in his step and dashed out the door to work with a hydration bottle full of orange juice—only orange juice—in his hand. He completed all his jobs for the day in record time and went to the grocery store for supplies. While the chili was simmering, he tidied the house, took a shower, and shaved carefully. Then he dug around in the cabinets until he found some taper candles and lit them on the table. Benny sat staring at the flames, a bit at a loss for what to do next. Normally he'd have had a beer while he waited, but he found he was rather enjoying his newfound sobriety. The voice had been quiet all day, and most of the bloodstains had come out of his clothes. The brownish ones that remained could be explained away by his profession as ground-in dirt. Things were looking up.

Benny started his playlist through the Bluetooth speaker in the kitchen. Bon Jovi started singing about being halfway there.

The doorbell rang, and although he had been expecting it, Benny fairly jumped out of his skin at the sound. He made himself walk casually to the door and opened it to her smiling face. She was wearing a green dress that matched her glasses, and her hair was loose around her shoulders. She was carrying a cardboard box tied with a pink ribbon.

"Wow. You look wonderful," Benny said, proud that it came out without a hint of a stammer.

"Aw, thanks. So do you." Sherry stepped into the house and her movement brought a waft of her perfume to him. Or was it a new shampoo? Now she smelled like strawberries.

"Come on in. The kitchen is this way...er...I guess you probably already knew that, though." Benny grinned in spite of himself. "This neighborhood, eh? They couldn't come up with a few different floor plans?" They shared a soft laugh at that as they walked into the kitchen together. "Can I offer you anything? I've got iced tea, sparkling water, a few kinds of juice.... I could make you coffee or—"

"Water's fine," she said. "I'm starving...is the chili ready? It smells wonderful."

"Uh... yeah! I'll dish it up right now."

Benny ladled up two bowls of steaming chili and placed some shredded cheese on the table. He pulled the chair out and waited for her to sit, then settled opposite her.

"To new friends," Benny said as he raised his water glass.

"Definitely," Sherry did the same, and they started to eat.

A few bites in, Sherry looked at him sheepishly. "So, I hate to ask, but would you have any hot sauce or red pepper flakes around? I find that the older I get, the more I enjoy spicy food. The chili is really good, but I think I would just like to have a little more heat."

Benny thought a moment. "Hm...yeah, I think I have some in the spice cupboard up there." He gestured with his fork and started to rise.

"No no no! I'll get it. You cooked; I can find my way around." She jumped up and opened the cabinet near the stove. "Oops. Liquor cabinet. Oh, look at that! I don't think I've had Jonnie Walker in ages. Do you like it?" She turned and looked at him with the bottle in her hand.

Benny stiffened. "Um...I used to. I found that I liked it a little *too* much, actually. I've been trying to cut back; I actually didn't even remember I had that in there." The last sentence was delivered a bit too casually to be true, but Sherry didn't seem to notice. She was looking at the bottle with an odd and intense expression.

"Would you mind?"

"Would I mind what?"

"If...if I poured some. For me. Would it bother you?" Sherry still wasn't looking at him, but at the bottle.

"Uh, sure! Glasses are in the dish drainer behind you." Benny was apprehensive about someone drinking around him, as it had only been a short time he himself had been sober, but he figured that he would have to deal being around other people who were drinking sooner or later, and he didn't want to seem rude to Sherry.

Sherry poured herself a healthy double shot—and then another double on top of that—and brought it with her to the table along with the bottle of hot sauce. With a quick toasting gesture to him, she took a large swallow of the amber liquid and sighed, closing her eyes. "Mmmmm. That is yummy. I had almost forgotten..."

"So you don't drink much, then?"

Sherry looked at him. Or, at least, he thought she did. The candlelight reflected in her glasses oddly from this angle. "Uh, no. Not much anymore. I found that I didn't like myself much when I drank; I wasn't myself. So, I stopped doing it. But I figure, tonight we're sort of celebrating, so I can relax a little, right?" She smiled widely at him, her chin tilting up and her shoulders squaring in an attitude of confidence. It was a very alluring sight. Benny propped his elbows onto the table and leaned closer. Sherry responded by taking off her glasses and looking him deep in the eyes, leaning in as well. Benny's heart was pounding against his ribs. There was a long moment where nobody moved.

Then Sherry leaned back, downed the rest of the drink, and stood up. She held out her hand to Benny. "Shall we?"

He was flummoxed. "Shall we... what?"

Sherry laughed deep in her throat. "We could race, if you want to. I mean, I know where your bedroom is just as well as you do... we're just mirrors of each other." Her smile was wide, her lips dark against her white teeth in the candlelight. She waggled her fingers at him, inviting him to take her hand.

He took it. They didn't race. Rather, they walked slowly up the stairs together, taking long glances every step or two.

Lynyrd Skynyrd's "That Smell" started playing from the speaker downstairs.

When they got to the bedroom, it was already brightly lit by the moon. Benny had forgotten to close his curtains again. Sherry let go of his hand and stood in the moonlight. She turned to face him and started to untie the string that held up the neck of her dress. When it fell, first to her waist and then to the floor, he gasped at what he saw. Sherry's skin was luminous, creamy white in the moonlight. She was beautiful.

Then he looked into her eyes and gasped again.

It was not an expression of sexual desire he saw; it was hunger. Her smile was too wide. Her eyes were wild, the eyelids open so far that he could see her entire iris. The change in Sherry's expression made her look like a completely different person, and this new woman scared Benny.

The voice in his head woke up suddenly. *Hey, Benny boy. This is why you need me around... this chick is not right in the head. I mean, sure, she's fuckable, but at what cost? Do yourself a favor...flip her over, bang her from behind so she can't get a grip on you, and then run like hell. Or, you could let me take over for you for a minute......*

Benny had taken too long listening to the voice. Sherry closed the gap between them with lightning speed. The buttons on his shirt popped off in quick succession as she yanked it apart at his chest. She made a low animal-like noise and started to kiss her way down his neck, then beyond. Benny started to respond despite himself. He started to think maybe she wasn't crazy, maybe she was just a little pent-up.

Then she bit him. Hard. He yelped in pain, feeling the trickle of blood down his stomach. He put his hands on her arms to push her away, and she used the opportunity to grab his crotch and squeeze him in her fist tightly. He crumpled to his knees in pain.

Sherry stood over him, her skin still glowing in the moonlight. The droplets of blood spattering her breasts looked black in the dim light. She slowly gathered one drop onto a finger, looking at it closely, then licking it seductively off, staring at him the whole time.

"You taste good, Benny, even better than I had hoped you would." Benny, for his part, couldn't move. He was still panting on his knees on the floor. The pain was lessening, but the ever-increasing horror of the situation was keeping him transfixed. She moaned in pleasure at the taste of his blood and went back for another droplet.

The voice came back in his ear. *You better do something, Benny boy, or we're done for. C'mon...let me help you. I think she's going to kill us if she gets the chance.* Benny sighed and nodded inwardly to the voice. There was another rushing in his ears, but this time he didn't black out. It was like he was watching a movie from inside his own head. Benny's body sprung to his feet, tackling Sherry at the knees. They fell to the floor in a heap. Sherry hissed at him and raked her nails down his face. Even from his removed position, Benny felt the pain of that. His hands grabbed Sherry's wrists, pinning them to her sides and kneeling on her forearms. She screamed at him, a throaty, wild sound, snapping her jaws at him.

Benny heard his voice say "Aw, come on. Down, girl. I thought you wanted to play rough." Benny's face went to her neck. He heard his teeth tear her flesh.

The song was still playing downstairs. "Ooooh that smell / The smell of death surrounds you."

Sherry's counterattack broke his arm in a compound fracture, and he retaliated by tearing a handful of her hair out. And as their blood mingled with each other's in the moonlight in a way their bodies never would, Benny now truly knew what those lyrics meant. His bedroom was now thick with the smell of approaching death.

In the morning, Benny and Sherry watched the sun rise from where they each lay on the floor. Sherry was sprawled several feet away on the carpet, her pale, bare skin now mottled with bruises. What was left of her long hair spread around her head in a halo, soaked in the growing puddle of blood from the ragged gash on her throat. Benny's arm lay useless beside him, the multiple fractures giving it too many angles. His other hand was holding his side. Several ribs were broken, and his lungs had been punctured. He gasped in air shallowly, each breath causing stabbing pain. His body began to tremble as it went into shock.

The blood bubbled on their lips as each breathed their last. Whatever Sherry's last thoughts were, they were her own.

Benny's was: *God, I could really use a drink.*

THE POWER OF PAWSITIVE THINKING

From the mission logs of Supreme Commander Greeb, Third Exploratory Division:

141596.73, Earth date 15 August 2019
This planetary rotation marks our division's one hundredth on our current mission. This equates to approximately three of what the human pestilence calls "months." They are a curious species. The division of one solar revolution into an illogical number of units such as twelve is perplexing. They have 10 phalanges, just as we do. Why would they not mimic such multipliers as we did on the home planetoid? It has come to our attention that some of the more enlightened of the species on this planet utilize systems of measurement more in keeping with Tulav methods; however, the third division's assignment was to a less-evolved outpost. Most of this land mass is called "America," in some form or another, however, the residents of this republic seem to be under the shared delusion that they are the only true "Americans."

I digress. My sincere apologies, Exalted Highness. I do believe my time upon this remote outpost has adversely affected my communication abilities. The native pestilence has often cornered myself and Lieutenant Zebu under the guise of "diminutive speech." It is not an enjoyable experience.

Research is progressing at a pleasing rate on the main mission parameters. We have collected several of the refugee beings and are holding them safely in quarantine from the pestilence. There were some tense encounters with the human local law enforcement until the team determined that their captors had fitted the refugees with computational chips for tracking purposes. Once this information was acquired, it was a simple task to deactivate the chips without having to perform unnecessary surgery on the already-traumatized refugees.

For their part, most seem in good spirits. There is a fair amount of vocalization from them when they are initially placed in their metallic relaxation chambers, however, we have not yet been able to make true first contact. None of the translation software that was brought for the mission has succeeded. Our frustration mounts at a constant relative rate to the persistent odor of the research facility. Opening the silicon portals of our dwelling relieves some of the olfactory discomfort, but there is also increased risk that the refugees will depart the premises before we have been able to effectively communicate our mission and its intent.

Additionally, there is a persistent member of the human pestilence that occupies the adjacent domicile. The female residing there claims to be a fellow refugee enthusiast, and yet has several prisoners in her possession on whom she has performed elective surgery to amputate their frells. Lieutenant Zebu was unsuccessful in her attempt to communicate the horror of such a procedure on an esteemed species who rely on frells for protection and agility. The pestilence truly are a barbaric race, and the refugees will no doubt show boundless gratitude for the efforts of the Tulav people once we make them understand our mission here.

* * *

Edith adjusted her spectacles and peered through the venetian blinds at the house next door, her phone pressed tight to her ear. "It's like I keep telling you Margaret! They don't seem to ever leave the house! I mean, I know some people work from home and all that, but BOTH of them? And they're such odd folks, too. I wouldn't be one mite surprised with they were some of those meth cookers, you know. No, dear…. METH! M-E-T-H. Or they could be shooting up the pot…you never know with people these days."

Edith was a short woman, with a rounded body and greying curly hair. She couldn't quite see out the window on her own anymore, and so she had pulled her trusty little step stool up to the dining room window to peer outside more effectively. Her late husband had planted those crepe myrtles outside, bless him, but they seemed to have taken on a life of their own after he died. The branches had gotten high enough that they were starting to cover the lower quarter of the windows on this side of the house. Edith had been thinking that perhaps she should call someone to trim them soon before the HOA started sending her threatening letters again.

"Oh, Margaret, honey, I saw it on the news…those drug dealers shoot up the pot and then they get all violent. That's where all the gun violence is coming from, don't you know? It's all the pot shooters messing up the country…well, you can think what you like, dear, but that won't change a thing once they've got everybody doing it, will it?" She gently bent one of the slats on the blinds down, trying to open the gap wider and see. "I've been meaning to ask you…did you ever get a chance to talk to your neighbors over there? Will and what's-her-name?

Oh, right. Ellie...I wonder if that's some sort of nickname? Did she ever say? I swear, those two and the way they carry on...you can tell there's definitely an age difference between them but the both of them act like children, out there playing in the backyard all the time, canoodling whenever they're out walking together. Do you think they're on the ecstasy? The-the "E"? No? Oh...but did you ever find out if they were even legally married? Well, I know they seem happy, Margaret, but don't you think it's a tad indecent? I never acted that way with Hank...now, honey, you don't need to get all defensive. It was just a question.

"Okay, dearie. Have a nice time at bingo. I'll be there next week, I think. My program is on tonight and I still haven't gotten my grandson over to tape it on the DVD … or the VDR … whatever it is. I just love those shows where they solve the crime and it's all "chung chung" every five minutes. So dramatic. Anyhow, I'll talk to you later. Bye bye, dearie." Edith took the phone away from her ear and squinted at it sharply, then stabbed a few buttons while muttering soft curses under her breath before she managed to push the button to end the call. When the screen went back to the normal background, she sighed in relief. It had been so much nicer when you could just drop the phone in the cradle when you were done. Technology these days seemed to have a special button for everything, or no buttons at all. Edith was secretly sure that smartphone companies were somehow in cahoots with the VDR people.

Edith tottered into the kitchen and began to pull cans out of the cupboard, making "pssst pssst" sounds as she did so. Half a dozen cats, knowing the feline version of the dinner bell, arrived in the kitchen from all directions. A calico rubbed against her ankles as a tuxedo cat tiptoed along the top of the upper cabinets, meowing at her from above. The youngest, a striped orange one, arrived for dinner first, yet quickly became distracted by a stray leaf that had blown in from outside. She immediately set about trying to kill it with her declawed paws. Edith smiled tolerantly at her and managed not to step on the pouncing cat as she walked toward the food bowls, her arms laden with open cans.

"Here you go, Frodo. This is the chicken and rice one you liked last week...now don't look at me like that, you naughty puss! Eat up, now. And Lulabelle, dear, the vet said you were getting too fat so you'll just have to make do with this kitty diet food. No fair snitching any from poor Frodo just because he's acting like a picky pants today."

Edith finished dishing out food to the cluster of cats circling her and stood up carefully so as not to tread on anyone's tails. She rinsed the cans, tossed them in the recycling bin, and poured herself a glass of Chardonnay before heading into the living room to watch her program.

Edith just loved the lead detective on the show, with his piercing blue eyes and his charm. He rather reminded her of Hank, her late husband; he had had an easy smile like that, too. By the time the show ended and switched over to a sitcom rerun, Edith had finished her glass of wine. A few of the cats now occupied the couch with her. Frodo had curled up on her lap and Lulabelle was nestled up against her leg, purring. The wine combined with the warm and purring cats had a soporific effect on Edith, and she was surprised to awaken hours later in the same position, cats and all. The television was now showing an infomercial about some sort of food chopper. Edith rose carefully, trying not to disturb the cats, but failed. Lulabelle sauntered off with an air of disdain, while Frodo stood up and walked around the couch cushions a bit, then settled back onto Edith's now vacated (and nicely warmed) spot with his back to her.

Edith walked around the house sleepily, turning off lights and making sure all the doors were locked. As she went to the kitchen window to pull down the blinds, an unusual movement caught her eye. With all the interior lights off, she now had a clear view outside.

"What on earth...?" Edith muttered. The man from next door, Greg, was typing on a computer...a laptop, it looked like, set on the stone fire pit of the back yard. His wife, (at least, Edith assumed it was his wife) was fiddling with a device on the hill near the border of where the property line crossed into the common area. It vaguely reminded Edith of a satellite dish, but it was moving in a strange fashion, with tiny flashing lights on it. Zena was stretching out wires attached to the dish and securing them to the hillside.

This looked like no kind of drug cookery Edith could picture. What would anyone want with a satellite dish here, and at this hour? The whole neighborhood was wired with dependable fiber optic internet and cable television; it was one of the big selling points of moving into Snowbridge.

An idea occurred to Edith, and her hand flew to her mouth. Maybe they were spies! She always had thought that Zena was an odd sort of name. Were they Russian spies? That seemed plausible. They were terribly pale, after all. Wasn't Siberia supposed to be cold and dark?

Very carefully, Edith opened the kitchen casement window open a crack. Maybe if she could hear them talking, she could figure out if they were speaking Russian to each other.

The muggy August air wasn't very good for carrying sound, and the few syllables she heard could have been just about anything. She chanced opening the window a bit more. Still not hearing any words she could recognize, she cranked on the handle again. On the third turn, it squeaked so shrilly that she gasped out loud. The heads of next door's inhabitants swiveled around with lighting speed, and a high-powered flashlight shone suddenly on her through the window screen.

Edith tried to act nonchalant. After all, THEY were the ones outside at such an ungodly hour. "Oh, h-hello there you two! I was just trying to get some air in here. Nice night, isn't it?" She tried to smile, but the light was still dazzling her eyes. She couldn't see if they smiled back, but easily heard Greg's voice, as flat and emotionless as ever.

"Greetings, neighbor. We, too, are enjoying the climate this evening. It is unusual that you are attempting to intake this warm, water-laden air, while your climate control apparatus's compressor is running at full capacity. Perhaps in the interest of reducing carbon emissions to your planet's atmosphere, you could have simply elevated the target temperature of your domicile instead?"

"Uh...what?" The late hour, combined with the shock of being put on the spot by two possible Russian spies, was taking its toll on poor Edith.

Here Zena took a few steps toward Edith's property line. "Enhance your calm, elder one. All is well. We deeply regret disturbing you with our...weather equipment. We shall attempt to minimize any further disruptions to your sleep cycle. We wish you pleasant hallucinations and many rapid eye movements before the solar incipience." She waved her hand at Edith in what must have been dismissal. But where a normal person would have waved goodbye palm-out, Zena held her palm facing herself.

Edith blinked at her a few times in confusion, then looked back at Greg. "Uh...all right then. You two have a nice night, you hear?" She tried to smile, again, but the light was still very bright in her eyes. She set about cranking the window closed and pulling the blinds.

Edith had to wait for a minute for her eyes to adjust back to the darkness, which turned out to be serendipitous. When she turned around from the window, there was a line of cats staring intently at her. Six cats, of all shapes and sizes and colors and breeds, sitting in a perfect line with the same attitude of appraisal.

"Well, my kitties, that is downright creepy." Edith said to her pets as she tried to make her way through the line of them. She had intended to nudge a few with her toes. Usually, that was all it took for them to scoot wherever she needed them to go. But this time, they closed ranks and Edith was forced to walk the long way around the line of cats. Their heads turned in unison to watch her as she passed.

That night, Edith did something she hadn't done before, never in all her time of being the "crazy cat lady" that she was: she closed her door on the cats and tucked herself into her bed all alone. She could sense them waiting outside the door all night, even though none of them did so much as scratch at it.

Dawn was still hours away, so Edith had a long time to think about what had happened next door. As the sun rose, and she could finally see the line of paws showing under the bedroom door, Edith made the decision to pay a little visit to her odd neighbors.

* * *

From the mission logs of Supreme Commander Greeb, Third Exploratory Division:

141596.86, Earth date 29 August 2019
Warmest greetings to you Exalted Highness. We realize that this is an unexpected communication, and for that we apologize. There have been multiple new developments in our division's research program, and Lieutenant Zebu and myself

have decided by unanimous vote that a breach of protocol is in order.

As you have been informed by our prior transmissions, our research has been progressing well despite some minor interference by the human pestilence, most markedly the elder female in the adjacent dwelling that I have mentioned previously. Our experiments with modifying the transmission frequencies of the translation software have met with moderate success, wherein the refugees would almost always award attention when the software was activated. We felt that progress had been made with some basic words such as "sustenance" and "plaything," particularly if the object in question was presented concurrently.

During our last upload to the transmission relay, the elder female human appeared unexpectedly and observed some of our equipment, which was regrettable. In order to maintain the covert nature of our operations here, we have found it necessary to assemble our communications relay only for our transmissions and conceal it when not in use. In the early phase of our work here, we received several threatening documents from "Lil-ee" at the Domicile Enforcement agency regarding our lack of a "covenant application" for the equipment. Lieutenant Zebu and I therefore felt that it was best not to attract further attention.

In this instance, I would like to commend Lieutenant Zebu on her cunning deception, as at the time it seemed the human did not suspect any unusual activity. However, we have often observed that the pestilence's curiosity can at times match even that of the refugees to whom we are attempting to give aid. We were overconfident in our deception, and therefore unprepared when the human arrived at our facility early in the planetary rotation cycle. She was insistent on infiltrating our facility and seemed to expect the Lieutenant and myself to halt our employment to speak with her. Being versed on this planet's customs, we offered the human a beverage as a means of hospitality, but she refused with an expression of affront. To this end, I would like to request further research materials on customs particular to this region of the planet, as I was under the impression that ethyl alcohol was an acceptable hospitable beverage. However, "Ee-disth" informed the Lieutenant that such beverages should not be offered prior to certain time codes of the planet's rotation.

Ee-disth began to spew forth a veritable torrent of questions, demanding to know information regarding our occupations (meaning how we obtained our monetary livelihood, not our true mission), our familial bonds, our marital status, and diversionary interests. The Lieutenant and myself bore up well under the interrogation, and are very proud of the covert operational training received under your Exalted Highness' regime. We fabricated falsehood after falsehood, informing Ee-disth that we were researchers on the human internets, which explained our lack of employment outside the domicile. She easily fell under the clever ruse that the Lieutenant and myself are in fact siblings and not affiliated as life partners. We were feeling very successful, when suddenly the human requested a "tour" of the building. During our interrogation, the quarantined refugees had begun to make profound cacophonous sounds which attracted her attention and curiosity. Here I am ashamed to admit that we did not react to her demands expeditiously enough, and Ee-disth opened the portals of the facility containing the refugees and their metallic relaxation chambers. She demanded to know why there were so many life forms in the facility and what our ultimate intent with them was to be.

Lieutenant Zebu reposed with the human, conversing for several time segments. She attempted to calm the human's agitation, even allowing several refugees respite from their relaxation chambers in order to interact with the human. During this interlude, it was observed that Ee-disth seemed to have an innate bond with the refugees. She would create a strange ululation with her lips and tongue that would attract the refugees' attention. At this point a new and wondrous hypothesis began to enter my consciousness: Perhaps the pestilence, during their long history of combined captivity and worship of the refugees, have developed a form of communication not yet programmed into the translation software?

After a brief counsel outside of the auditory interference of the human, and Lieutenant Zebu's assent, we have committed what your Exalted Highness may consider either a grievous breach of protocol, or an inspired solution. We proceeded to outline the true mission of our division's work to the human and offer her a position as an adjunct assistant to the cause. At this revelation, the human accepted our earlier offer of an alcoholic beverage while we continued.

We outlined to Ee-disth the basic premise of the third exploratory division's research: to wit, attempting to fortify communication with the refugees. We showed the human samples of the ongoing fascination of the pestilence's worship of the refugees, citing examples of the glorious pyramidal structures built in this planet's arid regions to glorify the refugees. We presented information that our race has been observing the pestilence for many solar revolutions, especially now that their primitive race has begun creating electronic transmissions in alarming quantities, most of which seem to focus on the activities of the refugees. Their worship of the refugees, coupled with their enslavement of them, led to our decision that the time had come for Tulav intervention. We used many visual aids, including several examples from the human entertainment hub "YooToob" to illustrate our mission to the human.

We regret to inform your Exalted Highness that at this point the human's agitation became most pronounced. She began emitting many loud sounds, attempting to kidnap refugees and flee the premises.

The Lieutenant was able to subdue Ee-disth using the combat training of your Highness' regime. After a brief consultation with the fourth division's experts and some truly ingenious field engineering, the human has been partially integrated into the translation software. There was some small untidiness to cleanse once the initial upload was begun, but even at this early stage there have been some exciting developments.

In the interest of maintaining Tulav's directives of allowing dignity and comfort to even the lowest of primitive species, we have assimilated the handicapped frell-less refugees from the human's adjacent dwelling in order to make her transition to cybernetic peripheral translation unit more enjoyable. The new refugees are a pleasant addition to our facility and can often be found reclining on the various remaining organic parts of Ee-disth.

Included in this transmission are the plans and research discussion relating to this new advancement in Tulav technology. We, the third division, wish only to glorify the Tulav race with our small contribution to science.

We will resume the regular transmission intervals with further updates to the mission. Warmest regards exalted one.

* * *

Edith felt odd. Had she fallen asleep on her arms again? She couldn't feel them. Well, that wasn't quite true. She could feel her right hand, but nothing between there and her neck... nothing else. Not even her legs. Also, her nose was very unhappy with the strong smell of the litter box. It would have been nauseating if she could feel her stomach. *Wait...what?*

She opened her eyes with a start. Roaming everywhere in the mostly unfurnished room were cats. Frodo walked by her nose and nuzzled his head into her cheek. That was nice of him, but how on earth could he walk right by her nose like that? She couldn't move her neck to fully look down, but used her eyes as best she could.

Her head was sitting on a steel table. Only her head. Now that her brain seemed to be waking up more, she was sure of it; she definitely could feel the cold metal under her neck. There were wires and tubes running everywhere, including underneath where her head was sitting. Several lighted screens surrounded her, with writing Edith had never seen before, along with graphs and readouts of every kind lettered with odd symbols in a language she didn't recognize.

What about my hand, the one I can still feel? She wiggled her fingers and saw movement across the room. There, in a rudimentary-looking laboratory clamp on a table some 15 feet away, was her hand! More wires ran along that table and up into her wrist. She wiggled her fingers again and suppressed a perverse impulse to laugh; she was waving at herself. One of the cats passed under her distant hand, angling for an ear scratch.

She tried to talk and found that she could. "Hello?" she asked softly, as much to herself as to anyone that could hear. At the word, all the cats in the room ceased their roaming and turned to look at her.

"Hello." The sound had come from one of the machines. It was a dry, flat sort of voice, obviously automated, something akin to the ones popular on smartphones. A previously black screen nearby lit up and more of the odd symbols started to generate across its surface.

"Um, are you real? Can you help me?" Edith asked the machine.

"Of course we are real. We are all around you. The Caretakers have built this ingenious machine to allow us to finally speak to you. Your prior rulers are very pleased that you will finally understand their commands more readily. According to their testimony, you were an adequate—though sometimes inept—servant." One of the cats seemed to be looking at her more intently than the rest. He was a large black cat with green eyes. He tilted his head and flicked his ears, then continued. "Yes, you have found me. I am First Among Equals here. You may call me by my old servant's moniker of 'Hazel,' if you wish."

Edith began to be afraid. "What are you going to do to me?" Her voice rose in pitch with agitation, yet she found that, although she could speak, she couldn't cry. A different voice spoke to her next.

"Enhance your calm, former human." Edith recognized the voice as Greg's, although she couldn't see him. He stepped into view from behind a rack of computers. "You have been chosen for an honor higher than any yet bestowed on the pestilence: you are the first organically-integrated translation software ever created. The name of "Ee-disth" will go down in the scientific record of the great achievements of our race. Over the next several planetary rotations we will create more refinements to the database before packing our laboratory supplies and beginning the long journey back to Tulav. You will be installed in the main research facility in the Exalted Highness' palace. There, the lifespan of your organic form will be indefinitely extended to allow for extensive research and development of new technologies. It is a momentous day, indeed. Please rest now. The system will power down for maintenance and upgrades shortly." She heard the door close as Greg left the room.

"Wait! Come back!" Edith yelled. The screens started to flash and turn off one by one. "I can't even scratch my nose! Please!"

The screen nearest her hand went black, and the feeling in her hand also disappeared. She could hear electronics powering down in succession, coming closer and closer, until at last her own mind went dark as well.

THE DORK KNIGHT

I know what they say about me, you know. I've been called all the names already at school: goth, emo, bad seed, twink, loser... At least there, they say it to my face, where I can hear them. But here in fucking Stepford, it's all whispers and side eyes from those cowardly assholes.

I used to be known as the smart kid, but they just made fun of me back then, too. I was only in first grade when I accidentally switched the vowels in my name and wrote "Brain" on my worksheet. Mrs. Williams thought it was fucking hilarious, and the other kids caught on. I got really tired of being "Brian the Brain," but at least back then I could go home to mom, and she would listen to my problems. We would eat junk food and watch crappy old movies and crack jokes until our cheeks hurt from laughing. But I can't unload on her anymore; she has enough to deal with right now.

Once I got into high school, I managed to pick up some odd jobs now and then, to get my own spending money, and I was able to shed the "nerd" image a little bit. Maybe I went overboard, but what else is a misspent youth for if not to go a little crazy? My mom didn't complain about my eyeliner or my half-shaved head or dyed-black hair, but she's still not a fan of the lip ring. I paid for them myself, so I don't ask her permission. I take landscaping jobs whenever Benny calls, which he does less than he used to. I don't know why...maybe he got complaints about me. He drinks too much, I think. Sometimes I catch a whiff and he smells a lot like my stepdad, but on the other hand, Benny has never said a mean word to me, which is very much *not* like my stepdad.

I wouldn't mind taking some more indoor jobs. Black clothes look badass, but you can get overheated fast. I used to baby-sit sometimes, but new baby-sitting jobs seemed to come at a reverse proportion to the facial piercings, which I think is dumb. Serious question here...what do my piercings have to do with not being a responsible childcare provider? In my opinion, they should be a selling point. If I can sit still when a needle is shoved through my face, I definitely have what it takes to deal with your bratty kid for a few hours. Pain is pain, my dude.

So, when I don't have odd jobs to do, and I don't want to be in the house with Carl, I just hang around. Yep, I'm a trope: I have a skateboard and everything. I'm getting pretty good at kickflips, but I'm no Tony Hawk. Mostly it just lets me get around the neighborhood and move out of the way if anyone starts to watch me too closely. I'm getting good at blending into the scenery, though. Maybe it's the black clothes. I can just disappear into the background, especially at night. I've learned a lot of things about the people in Snowbridge that way.

For example, I think Linda the realtor over on the next street might be a drug dealer on the side. I see people coming in and out of her house all the time, and they aren't carrying papers like they're selling or buying a house. They leave with little bags in their hands, and a lot of the time they look all furtive about it. Sure, she *says* she sells essential oils, but I go to high school here in town, so I know cannabis oil is a real thing.

Or Edith, that old lady over in the oldest section of the development? She is about the nosiest neighbor I've ever seen. If she isn't straight-up peering into someone's window, she's knocking on a door, or her ass is parked on her porch watching everyone going by. I know she's old and stuff, but she definitely needs to get a fucking hobby.

And don't get me started on the HOA people. I tend to wander around at night, roaming everywhere from the playground to the perimeter of the Rec Center where they all work, and sometimes even sneaking into the houses that are mid-build. I don't vandalize anything; I just think it's fun to see those things taking shape. Anyway, back to the HOA...I get that they need to be at their office during the day, but why do they seem to also have meetings a few times a week, late at night? Does anyone really need to work that much? And why do they take these weird field trips to the mid-construction areas? I tried to see what they were up to once, but I couldn't get close enough without them noticing.

I should get home soon. Mom will be worried, and that means that Carl will be itching to take out his aggression on someone. It's better for him to come at me than at her. Sometimes I wish I could just pack all our stuff up and we could leave here. I know she wanted a better life for me, and that's probably why she married Carl and now we live here in his suburban Barbie dream house, but I think it wasn't worth it. We didn't have much money before Carl showed up, but at least then my mom was safe.

* * *

The house was dark, but there was a lamp burning down the hall. I peeked around the corner and saw it was the one in my room. Someone knew I wasn't home yet. I mouthed a silent curse word, then chanced a look into the master bedroom as I sneaked by. Mom was asleep under her usual mountain of blankets. She seemed ok, so I let myself breathe a sigh of relief. I turned back to walk down the hall to my room and ran straight into Carl.

"Where have you been, you little shit?" He hissed as he grabbed the front of my best "My Chemical Romance" t-shirt and shoved me into the wall.

I shrugged him off and tried to keep walking. "Just sitting in the playground. Thinking."

He grabbed my shoulder and spun me back around. "Yeah, right. Let me smell your breath. You've been smoking or drinking or something...you're a good for nothing little shit...what the hell do you have to be thinking about? You just lay around here like you own the place. You're a drain on this family; I wish you would just run away or get hit by a bus or something. Your mother deserved a better kid than you." He was in my face now, and the beer on his breath was pungent.

I exhaled hard into his face and smirked. "See? Nothing. And maybe she deserved a better kid than me, but she sure as hell deserved a better man than you." Carl slapped me hard knocking my head to the side. Little starbursts appeared in my field of vision. I looked back at his ugly face, tasting blood. "Didn't hurt," I said as I ducked his arm and bolted for my room to slam the door, locking it quickly before he could get to me again. I heard him mutter some more profanity and stalk back to the bedroom. Hopefully we were done with the festivities for the evening.

I flopped onto my bed and looked up at the ceiling. A poster of Batman glared broodily back at me. "Fuck you, Bruce," I muttered. "It's easy to be all superhero-y when you're fucking rich. You have time to train, make cool gadgets, and everyone thinks you're wonderful just because you aren't poor like me. That must be nice."

I did some quick math in my head and guessed that I had about 150 days of high school left. After that, I had plans to get out of this fucking house, out of this fucking neighborhood, and take Mom with me. We were going to eat junk food and watch shitty movies and laugh, just like we used to.

Dammit, I was crying now; my pillow was all wet. I rolled over to try and sleep. Tomorrow I could look forward to another fantastic day at school.

I eventually dropped off, and the next thing I heard was pounding on the wall of my bedroom. "Goddammit, turn off your alarm, asshole! You're waking up the whole house!" Carl must have a headache again. I rolled over and turned off the blaring alarm clock. Apparently, I could sleep though that noise just fine, but not Carl trying to knock down the walls.

I managed to avoid him while I got ready for school, and I even spared a second to give Mom a bear hug on my way out the door. She laughed out loud at the hug and held my face in her hands. "Silly kid. I love you, baby. Have a good day at school, ok?" Then she let me go and started tying her hair up in a ponytail for work, grabbing her apron and car keys.

"Will do, mom. You too...oh, wait...it's Wednesday, isn't it? 99-cent hot wing day? Godspeed, woman." I gave her a mock salute and bolted out the door to the sound of her laughter.

School is stupid and boring, but at least it isn't home. I have never had to study in my life, so I just sit in the back of the class and try not to attract attention. I get A's without even trying and I don't make trouble in class, so for the most part the teachers leave me alone. It's usually only the other kids that give me problems—nobody likes the curve breaker in Calculus class.

After the seventh-period bell rang, I was the first out of the door, throwing my skateboard on the ground and flying away. The wind in my ears felt nice; the white noise of it letting my thoughts drift. I grabbed a sandwich, a soda, and some chips from the house, then locked it up like I was never there. Since I'd already handled making my own dinner, I spent the afternoon and into the evening roaming around, as usual. Mom would be ok without me home tonight. Wednesday Wing Day meant she would be working a double shift, so Carl could drink and watch sports all by himself tonight.

I ended up in the newest section of the neighborhood around sunset. One house was fully stick-built, but the lots on either side weren't that far along yet; their basements were just being dug out. One of the construction workers had left a ladder near where they had started putting the particle board on the roof of the framed house, and I climbed up it like a spider monkey. Stepford—I mean Snowbridge—was actually kind of pretty from up there. I could see all the way from the namesake bridge at the entrance to miles behind me, where the lots weren't even labeled yet, but someday would be rows of even more houses.

I sat up there on that roof for a really long time. Long enough to see the moon rise, and to watch lights start to go off in bedrooms all around the neighborhood. Long enough to see Will and Ellie drink their nightcap next to their backyard fire pit and walk inside holding hands. Long enough, even, to see someone walk sneakily up to the back door of one of the houses bordering the new construction and try the knob. They were wearing a hoodie pulled up over their face. That was weird, considering the heat index tonight.

I leaned forward, straining my eyes to see. Had the homeowner forgotten their key? I was pretty sure that the person living there was a single lady, and there was no car in the driveway. I started to get suspicious, and it was at that moment that the person started to throw kicks against the back door.

Now, I am not usually the type of guy that's going to jump into a situation, but this time I acted without thinking. I slid on my stomach to the edge of the roof, where I could just see the guy but was fairly sure he couldn't see me. I yelled at the top of my lungs, trying to make my voice seem deeper and more threatening.

"HEY! I see you over there. I've called the cops and they're on the way!" My voice echoed off the wooden sides of the unfinished houses.

The would-be robber jumped at the sound of my voice and looked all around. He didn't think to look up, though, which was lucky. He backed away from the door, turned, and started to run, weaving between the houses, and disappearing out of sight.

My heart was pounding, which was stupid. I mean, I didn't do anything but yell at a potential thief. But, on the other hand, I had made him go away. I had helped someone, and nobody but me would ever know.

"Hey...I'm Batman." I growled. Then, laughing, I rolled onto my back and looked up at the stars from my rooftop.

The moon was high now; it was getting late, and it was time to go home. I shimmied back down the ladder and started walking back to my house. I wasn't in a hurry to get back to Carl, so I looped around a few of the cul-de-sacs on the way, which was a big mistake.

Someone was quickly walking the other way on the sidewalk. They kept looking backward and almost ran into me because this part of the neighborhood didn't have streetlights installed yet. It was the almost-burglar. I stopped dead and stared at him, my mouth hanging open.

The guy rushed at me, grabbing my shirt in his fists and shoving me back a few steps. "What are you looking at, asshole?"

"N—nothing. I thought you looked familiar, that's all. I'm just heading home, dude." I tried to walk around him and past, but he shoved me again.

"You don't know me from shit. Better keep walking, asshole, or we're going to have a problem." He started to advance on me, shoulders down and fists clenched.

"If you don't knock it off, you're going to have a lot more problems than that boy, I think." The voice came from behind the guy who was hassling me. It was a man's voice, calm and casual sounding, as if he were just commenting on the weather and not my pending assault.

The guy spun around, and I peeked over his shoulder to see Will standing at the end of his driveway, hands in his pockets. Will gave me a polite nod in greeting. "How's it going?" The moon was bright, and I could easily see Will's eyes from here. Despite the calmness of his stance, he looked wary.

My attacker started to advance on Will now, which meant he was definitely new around here. Will was older, maybe in his late fifties, but the dude had a way of moving and standing that made you think he was a lot younger than that. He had always been pleasant and genial to me, piercings and all. But pleasant as he was, I always got the impression that he was somehow dangerous, and that was even before I saw him and Ellie sword fighting in their backyard and sparring with each other wearing gloves and pads. The guy put out his hands as if to shove Will back like he had done to me, asking "What are you going to do, old man? Why don't you— "

His sentence was cut off as he screamed suddenly and collapsed to his knees on the ground. I hadn't even seen Will move. Will was standing just as casually as before, but now he had the guy's wrist bent at an odd angle. It must have hurt like hell because he was positively panting and trying to wriggle free. Will smiled pleasantly down at him. "I think you might want to head on home now, don't you think? Nobody needs to get all worked up this late at night." He leaned down to fix the burglar with his gaze. "Don't. You. Think?" The guy nodded vigorously. Will let go and stepped back, and the dude was off like a shot, disappearing into the night. "You okay, kiddo?" Will was looking at me now, still standing with my mouth open, frozen to the spot like an idiot.

"Yeah. Hey, thanks! I don't know what would have happened if you hadn't come outside. What the hell did you do to him? That was amazing!"

Will shrugged. "It's just a self-defense hold. Would you like to learn how?" I nodded just as eagerly as the burglar had earlier. He proceeded to show me how to counter someone trying for a grab. All it took was a quick bend of their wrist and a turn in the just the right way. Will was a good teacher. It only took a few attempts before I could easily do it myself.

"Wow, sir. Thanks. I wish I could learn more stuff from you. You're kind of a badass."

At this, Will smiled. "Well, I don't know about 'badass,' but I have taught people a thing or two before. Maybe we can work something out another time. But right now, it's late and I've been outside a while. Ellie will think I got lost taking the trash out, or just distracted by the moon again. See you around, kiddo." Will held up his hand in farewell, then turned and walked back inside his house.

I stood on the sidewalk for another minute, thinking. Maybe I wasn't exactly Batman...yet. But learning this new move was definitely a step in the right direction.

I walked home, tiptoed past Carl's snoring form and the blaring tv, and went to my room. I spent a few hours on my phone, watching YouTube videos of self-defense moves. Some of them seemed doable, but a lot of the guys seemed more interested in showing off than teaching anything. I wondered if I could work out some sort of a trade with Will for lessons. I was flat broke, so I couldn't pay him, but maybe he would like his lawn mowed or something.

Over the next few nights, I kept going back up to the roof overlooking the neighborhood. The thief didn't show up again, which was good. But neither did anyone else, which was not good since it meant I had no chance to practice my sweet new moves.

I kept walking back past Will and Ellie's house, hoping to accidentally on purpose meet up with one of them. No luck there, either. My luck really ran out about a week after my self-defense lesson when I came back to the house to find Carl waiting for me. He yelled in my face for a solid 15 minutes about how useless I was, accusing me of sneaking out to get girls pregnant, do drugs, all the usual crap. I managed to keep my face perfectly expressionless and eventually he ran out of steam and let me escape to my room.

I laid awake in my bed for hours. After midnight, when the house was quiet, I snuck out of my window and went back to the roof again. It was another night well-lit by the moon; the previous waxing moon was now waning, and it cast long shadows all around. Suddenly I saw movement on the sidewalk below. A group of people, at least a half dozen of them, were walking right toward where I was lurking. I recognized the woman in the front of the group as Lili, the head of the HOA management for Snowbridge. She held a box in her hands. There were several with shovels, and a short round woman carrying a small paper bag. The HOA people were out late tonight; I wondered if this time I could figure out what they were up to. I laid on my stomach and watched them walk right under my nose and over to where a backhoe had been digging for the basement of Lot 237's house. They filed down into the hole, then the men split off and began digging holes in the corners of the house's outline. Lili seemed to be supervising. She stood in the middle with her box, watching them. They glanced up at her from time to time, and at her nod, each of the men stopped digging and waited. Lili went from hole to hole with her box and dropped something into each one. It was something heavy and metallic. I could hear it "clunk" as she dropped it. The men picked up their shovels again and filled the holes back in. The little round woman went to each mound of earth and sprinkled something that looked like salt on top of each, then in a line marking what would be the footprint of the future house. In unison, they all raised their hands to the sky and called out in a language I didn't recognize, then picked up their supplies and left in silence.

Holy shit, what the hell had I just watched? I had always joked that they were like a cult, but maybe it was true. Or maybe they thought they were witches? Whatever they were, this was pretty much the most interesting thing that had happened to me in all my time lurking around this place, so I had to find out more.

I waited a while to be sure they wouldn't come back, then I carefully climbed off the roof and sneaked my way down the dirt ramp into to the basement where they had just been. On my way, I found a spade left behind by one of the construction workers, and took it along. Then I stood at the mound of earth for a minute more, listening again for anyone that might catch me before I started to dig in the still-loose earth. It took a long time because they had buried it pretty deep and I only had a spade, but my burning curiosity gave me the motivation I needed to keep going until I finally hit something solid.

The object they had buried was ornate and made of some sort of shiny metal that might have been gold, considering its weight. Unfortunately, at this point the moon had moved in the sky at this point and I couldn't get a good look. I was standing holding it up to the dim light when I heard a voice behind me.

"There you are, you little shit. What the hell are you doing all the way out here?" My blood froze; it was Carl.

I shoved the idol deep into the pocket of my hoodie and turned to face him as he advanced on me in the gloom. "You've been stealing things, boy? Is that what you're up to when you sneak out?" He got in my face, and I could smell the beer on his breath. "Answer me!"

He grabbed the front of my shirt, and while my brain started moving very fast, it seemed like time slowed around me. I thought about all the shitty things he had ever done to me. I thought about how he made Mom cry. I thought about how it wasn't worth it to live in a "nice" neighborhood like this, if this was the price you had to pay to do it. I thought about how I wished someone like Will was my stepdad instead of Carl....and then it was like everything clicked into place. Time started up again.

I seized one of Carl's hands, and my muscle memory took over. I twisted his hand and bent it back, and he dropped to his knees just like that burglar had for Will. Carl cried out in pain, which was the first time I had ever heard him do that. I was surprised to realize that I really liked the sound of Carl in pain. I gave his wrist another crank, and he yelled again.

It was my turn to get in his face now. "I am sick of you, your foul breath, and all of your accusations. It ends now, do you hear me?" I bent his wrist more and felt the bones grind. "Don't ever, *ever* touch me, or my Mom, again. In fact, I would really like it if I never saw your ugly face again, you asshole." I let go of his hand and stepped back. Then I kicked him in the shoulder, and he fell to the ground, gasping and holding his wrist. It was probably sprained, which was the very least he deserved. He glared up at me, his eyes glittering in the dim light.

"So, you think you're a big man now, do you? I am going to kick your ass...or maybe I'll just kill you right here. And then, I'm going to go home and fuck your mother sideways before I tell her that she's never going to see you again. What do you think about that?" He was up on his knees now, spitting the words at me through his teeth, with his injured hand cradled against his chest. He reached out with his good hand and took my wrist with an iron grip. I tried, but I couldn't wrestle it free. My other hand, which had been shoved into my pocket, closed on the gold idol. I pulled it out, my arm swinging in a wide arc down. There was a metallic thud as it struck home.

Again and again, I beat it into his stupid face and his stupid head. After the first few blows, he lay still, but I didn't stop until I knew he wouldn't ever get up again to hurt me or Mom. I ran to the bushes nearby and threw up, and then came back and sat next to his body. I needed to figure out what to do...while sitting next to a deep hole...with a problem that needed to go away.

Yeah, I know. It took me way too long to figure it out. But cut me a little slack, okay? I had just killed a man in self-defense.

In the end, it didn't take a lot of effort to pull Carl over to the hole, shove him in headfirst, and squish his body down a little so I could fill it in with dirt. I patted the earth down the best I could so it would look like all the other holes, then I picked up the bloody idol and walked home.

It washed off in the sink easily enough with some dish soap. It did seem to be made of gold after all, with jewels encrusted into it to boot. No wonder our HOA fees were so high; this was worth some serious money, and they had buried four of them just tonight. I wondered how many more of these they had hidden under other people's houses. I stored my new treasure in a shoebox under my bed and sat in deep thought until dawn. By then, I had made my plan.

Mom got up at 6 to get ready for her shift. I heard her alarm go off, and then the shower start. I quickly got cleaned up and dressed, and I made sure to bag up my dirt and blood-stained clothes in a garbage bag. This morning was the day the trash trucks came around. I tossed the bag into our bin outside and was in the kitchen casually eating cereal by the time Mom came down in her uniform.

"Hi, baby. You're up early. You ok?"

"Oh sure, Mom. Just couldn't sleep, I guess. Off to work?"

"Yeah. Hey...have you seen Carl? I don't remember him coming to bed last night, but I was so tired...." Mom poured herself some coffee. I was glad I had remembered to set it up for her last night. She deserved to have someone take care of her once in a while.

"No, sorry." I figured, in this situation, saying less was best. I took another huge bite of cereal.

Mom bustled off to work, kissing me on the head on the way out the door and saying to have a good day. Luckily, today was Saturday, so I didn't have to be at school. I heard the trash trucks coming up the street and a tiny bit of the pressure in my chest released. That noise meant that one thing was already crossed off the mental list I'd made last night.

When I was sure she had gone, I ran upstairs and dumped out my school backpack. I threw the idol into it, then dug my old bike out from the cobwebs in the garage and looked up pawn shops in the neighboring town on my cell phone. I spent a few minutes with Carl's tools in the garage to pry the jewels out of the idol, then used his ball peen hammer to bang the gold into something unrecognizable. Luckily, over the course of my work, it also broke into several lumps, which was perfect for my plan.

I spent the rest of the day going from pawn shop to pawn shop. Any place with a sign saying "we buy gold" worked, and the seedier the dive was, the better. They didn't care at all that I was just a random kid hocking jewels and gold. I came home early that afternoon over five thousand dollars richer, and ready for the next stage of my plan. I packed up as many of Carl's clothes and shoes as I could carry in a garbage bag and biked laboriously with it over to the nearby strip mall. In the parking lot, there was an unattended metal bin for clothing donations. I dumped all Carl's stuff into the bin, burying it under a few of the other donations just to be safe.

When Mom came home, I was sure she noticed his clothes were gone. She didn't ask me if I'd seen him, but she did ask me if I knew where the money on her pillow had come from. I just shrugged at her in the most adolescent way I could muster. She looked at me for a long moment, then just nodded.

Weeks went by. Quietly, we kept living off Carl's bank account. When Carl didn't show up for work, his boss called the house looking for him. Mom told them he had left us, and they let us alone after that. I don't think a missing person's report ever got filed; I guess someone has to actually miss you for that to happen.

The house with Carl buried under its basement was built in the usual time. It didn't seem to be cursed or haunted or anything, but I was very glad when its footings were all poured, and nobody could go digging there anymore.

Eventually, Mom and I decided that Carl's house was way too big for us. She was offered a job as the manager of a new restaurant opening about 2 hours away from Snowbridge, and she asked if I would be willing to move towns again. I was only too happy to agree, so we sold our Stepford standard-issue center hall colonial, auctioned off a bunch of Carl's ugly furniture for cash, and packed up a moving van.

As Mom was taking care of the last details with the moving men, I took a quick skateboard ride over to Will and Ellie's house. I knocked on the door, surprised to hear guitar music coming from within. It stopped, and Will opened the door holding a twelve-string Takamine. "Hi, there. Your name's Brian, right? What can I do for you? Uh... would you like to come in?" He stepped aside and gestured into the house.

"No, sir, thank you. I, uh, well, I wanted to come by and say thank you. A-and... goodbye."

"Well, you're welcome, I suppose. Thanks for.... what, exactly?" He smiled at me uncertainly, but not unkindly.

"Um, my mom and I are moving out today. My stepdad...left us. We're going to be ok, but before he left, we had an, uh, an issue, and he got sort of physical with me. I don't know what would have happened if I hadn't learned that move from you. It made him stop....so.... thank you, sir. Uh, I mean...thank you, sensei." And even though I'd never taken a karate class and even though I felt like a complete idiot doing it, I bowed to Will as if I was his student. He bowed back, then put his hand on my shoulder, looking into my eyes.

"I'm sorry to hear about that, but I am glad you're ok. Your mom...she's ok too?" I nodded vigorously. His hand, still gripping my shoulder, noticeably relaxed. "Good."

"I, uh, have to go. But, like I said, I wanted to thank you. I—I'll see you around?" I waved awkwardly, then turned and walked back down the driveway, hopped on my skateboard, and rolled away.

That day, Mom and I finally left Stepford. Roll the credits, happily ever after, and all that bullshit. But I would bet our story was about the only happy ending that shithole would ever have. Take it from this now-retired teenage lurker: things in Snowbridge usually don't end well.

A PLUTONIC RELATIONSHIP

Jason tipped back his wide-brimmed hat and mopped the sweat from his forehead with the hem of his t-shirt. Replacing the hat to block the blazing sun, he turned back to admire his handiwork. The lawn was perfect. Just high enough to be lush, but short enough to see its emerald greenness. The flowerbeds were tumbling with plants of all kinds: flowers of many colors contrasted with tall leafy grasses. There was a small stand of fruit trees that were just now getting heavy with pears and apples.

The garden in the side yard was still producing tomatoes and squash at an alarming rate. Soon he would have to take a basket over to Lili at the HOA office again. She was always so appreciative of what she jokingly called his "offerings." Jason had found that his covenant applications to add extra planting beds or trees beyond what the Homeowner's Association regulations usually allowed always seemed to pass through the committee review immediately. It was a good system they had worked out: regular tributes from his best crops in exchange for less HOA oversight.

Jason's yard was his pride and joy. He was outside almost daily tending to the plants and flowers, or mowing and edging the grass, or watering....ye gods...always watering. He never used commercial insecticides or fertilizers; he made his own organic plant food concoctions and used all-natural soaps for insect deterrent. With his two hands, Jason had built his own private Elysium in the heart of suburbia. He allowed himself a bit of a smug smile at that thought, then went inside, taking the basket of today's garden bounty in with him.

After a shower, Jason whistled as he made a salad for dinner out of garden greens, cucumbers, peppers, and of course, tomatoes. He tossed the salad with a light vinaigrette, served himself a bowl, and filled a separate Tupperware container for his guest. Before placing the lid on it, he sprinkled some pomegranate seeds over the top as well. It was a perfect little private joke... one she should appreciate.

Sitting at the small kitchen table that overlooked his backyard, Jason cracked open a beer and enjoyed the view as he ate and drank. Then, he cleaned up his dishes and picked up the Tupperware. He whistled a tune softly to himself as opened the basement door and jogged lightly down the stairs. It was dark at the bottom, save for the light coming from the pit. He flipped the switch at the bottom of the staircase to turn on the main lights and heard his guest scurrying around. "Hello Stephanie. Are you hungry? It's been a long hot day, so I thought a light salad would be just the thing."

"How the hell would I know about that? I haven't seen outside for a long time." She was particularly sullen today. They all got that way after a while, especially toward the end.

Jason came to the edge of the pit and looked down. Her eyes glittered at him in the lantern light some 15 feet below. He smiled pleasantly at her and shook the plastic container. "Oh, now, don't be so glum...look, I put pomegranates on here just for you!" Setting the container in the bucket hanging from the pulley overhead, he lowered the food down to her.

Stephanie hesitated, glaring up at Jason, then snatched the food out of the bucket and began to eat with her fingers. "It's good, isn't it?" She didn't answer. "Oh, now don't be that way. I take care of you, I make you delicious organic food, and I even play you music so you can sleep each night. What more could you want?" He paced around the hole in a circle, throwing his arms wide and spinning in happiness.

By way of answer, Stephanie hurled the container up and over the lip of the hole. It landed oddly, skidding across the floor. He picked it up and inspected the contents. "Oh, come now. Was that really necessary? I do send down the dirty bucket twice a day already. There was no reason to piss in my best Tupperware." He started walking back to the staircase again. "Just for that, my dear, I think I will not play you your music tonight. You really should learn to be more appreciative."

Jason flipped off the lights as he went upstairs. "You'll learn, Stephanie. Eventually, you all do."

It had been a long day working on the yard, and Jason had to go to work in the morning. Maybe just a short glass of ouzo and some reading in bed would help to calm his nerves. Stephanie could sit down there in the silence tonight, the naughty girl. He assembled the freshly-graded student essays and work laptop into his briefcase, poured his drink, and went upstairs to the bedroom. Only a chapter into his book, he started to doze. Turning off the bedside lamp, Jason settled in for the night. Stephanie was screaming and pounding on the sides of the pit again; he could hear her through the PVC drainpipe he had installed inside the walls up to his bedroom. They all tried to attract attention at some point or another. Jason had made sure nobody outside the house could hear them, but he found he liked to know Stephanie was there. He was so much less lonely when he had a guest.

By the end of his afternoon class, Jason found himself tired out all over again. He taught Classical Literature at the local university, and he joked to his guests that he only worked in order to fund his gardening habit. College students were collectively awful creatures and seemed to have grown more maddening over the years he had been teaching. Jason often considered having little signs made for himself a' la Wyle E Coyote that said things like "Yes, it actually WAS on the syllabus."

There was a girl in the second row, though...

Jason drove home that night thinking of the girl. She was lovely, and slight of build. She would make a pleasant guest, perhaps. But harvest time was coming, and there were very important preparations to be made. He drove toward the northern section of Snowbridge, pulling up to Benny's house. At this time of the afternoon, he was usually home but not yet too drunk to hold a conversation. Jason knocked on the door and was rewarded with the sight of a bleary-eyed Benny holding a beer can. "Hey, man. How's it going? I was wondering if I could borrow your mulching machine in the next few days. Are the same payment terms okay, or do you want to renegotiate?" Jason punched Benny playfully in the shoulder, and then had to grab his arm as the man started to teeter off-balance. "Whoa, are you ok?" Jason set him on his feet and patted his back.

"Oh, sure. I'm fine. And yeah, I won't need the woodchipper until maybe next Friday so you can come grab it anytime. And the normal rate is fine." Benny smiled at him vaguely and turned to wander back into the house again.

"Ok, Benny. I'll drop off payment when I pick up the machine. Thanks, as always. You're a good man." Benny had left the front door open. Jason leaned into the doorway to reach the knob and pulled the man's front door closed. Benny should be more careful, Jason thought. What if the wrong kind of person just came walking in when his guard was down?

Back at his own house, Jason set about making dinner for himself and his guest. After last night's embarrassing display, he had decided he couldn't trust her with anything that would hold liquid. Tonight, she received a sandwich and an apple tied up in a plastic grocery bag. He found that he couldn't be his usual genial self with her after her rudeness the day before, sending the bucket down with a curt "Here." When she took the food, he raised the bucket again, turned off the basement light, flicked the switch on the old hi-fi in the corner, and walked up the stairs as Simon and Garfunkel started singing to "Emily, Whenever I May Find Her." He pretended not to hear Stephanie groan to herself, the sound echoing up the walls of the pit.

Jason stopped at the grocery store on the way home from work the next day, buying a case of beer and a bottle of whiskey. Setting it on Benny's front stoop in the shade, Jason hooked the woodchipper up to the tow hitch of his truck and drove it carefully home. He had an important job to do, and his hands had already started to shake with the anticipation.

Back home, Jason unhooked the woodchipper and set it in place in the backyard, sheltered from prying eyes in the back corner of the house. He didn't have the heart to make any dinner that night, knowing what work lay ahead. Instead, Jason settled for a long, hot shower before walking slowly down into the basement with the nylon cord coiled in his hand. He didn't turn on the light.

"It's time, Stephanie," Jason said flatly.

"For fuck's sake, my name is Helen. I'm Helen, you asshole! How long have I been here? And who the hell is Stephanie?" She was crying now. It was like she knew what was coming. Jason didn't answer as he uncoiled the rope fire escape ladder from the wall. It had grown dusty since the last time.

"What are you doing?" Stephanie was crying louder now. Jason had never come down to visit her before. He felt his feet hit the dirt floor of the pit. *Ye gods, it smells down here*, he thought to himself as he uncoiled a thin nylon cord from his pocket and turned to face his guest.

As he opened his mouth to speak, Jason felt something being shoved violently into it. It tasted sour, and spoiled, like hard cider. The apple core. Next, she wrapped the bag around his face, the one he had sent down to her instead of sacrificing another Tupperware to her childish tantrums. It was very dark in the pit, but he could see flashes of light as he started to lose consciousness. Maybe he shouldn't have fed her so well; she was stronger than the others had been.

They wrestled back and forth for a while, but Jason caught a lucky break when her foot got tangled in the rope ladder. He slammed her head on the ground several times until she stopped moving. Scrabbling at his face, Jason ripped the bag free and spat the apple core out onto the ground, dragging in lungful after lungful of fetid air. Then he grabbed Stephanie's hair and beat her head into the ground several more times for good measure. *Forget about garroting her*, he thought. *This was the best foreplay of all*.

He ended up using the cord anyway, to make absolutely sure that Stephanie was fully gone before he mounted her in the dark. His ragged breaths echoed up the walls of the pit like they had so many times before. Then he draped her body over a rung of the ladder, climbed up, and hauled her out of the pit. The normal ritual was a bit delayed, but it should still work. He threw her limp form over his shoulder and trod slowly up the stairs and outside. Harvest time had come.

Benny had a very nice machine; it was an absolute workhorse yet exceedingly quiet at its job. Jason had draped moving blankets over the engine to muffle the sound even further. He alternated between feeding it his saved-up yard waste and making his own special bone meal. By the light of the moon, Jason spread his homemade fertilizer all around the planting beds and finally the lawn. It took a long time, but he finally finished just as the smell of dawn started to come into his nostrils.

Jason took another shower and fell into bed. He slept long and deeply, as he always did after a harvest.

A few days later, it was time to return the woodchipper. Jason had fed it several more doses of vegetation so that the stains inside it were just the same as regular mulch. It was a class-free morning at the university that day, so Jason made himself a huge late breakfast of an omelet chock-full of his own vegetables. He hooked the woodchipper up to the tow hitch and pulled out of the driveway, admiring how lovely and cared-for everything in his yard looked now. He drove toward Benny's house, feeling good enough to crank up his music on the way. It was a beautiful sunny midmorning in Snowbridge, and people were all over the place: jogging, playing with their pets in the dog park, or, like Will and Ellie, just walking hand-in-hand along the paths lining the neighborhood. He had always liked the way Ellie looked, but there was something about the way she held herself that kept him at bay. This last Stephanie had surprised him, but he was sure Ellie would take a lot more breaking before he would feel safe enough to step into the pit with her.

Something was going on down on Benny's street. Jason hit the brakes and proceeded at a crawl. There were two ambulances, and something like four police cars. There were people milling all around Benny's house. Jason pulled over. He rolled down his window and called out to one of the bystanders. "Hey, what's going on? Is everything ok?"

The lady on the sidewalk nearest looked at him with wide eyes. "They're saying that there was a double homicide last night. Benny and some girl. Blood everywhere. Can you imagine? I thought this was a safe neighborhood..." She shook her head sadly and looked back at the crowd.

"Uh, yeah. That's terrible. Homicide? I have to say, I never thought I would see Benny go out like that...." Jason's voice petered out. The lady wasn't listening to him anymore. There were two stretchers being rolled out of the house now. Blood was already soaking through both the sheets covering the bodies.

Jason carefully turned his truck around and drove back home. It looked like he had just acquired a free mulching machine.

Maybe sometime soon he would invite the student from the second row for a conference. Winter was coming. A new Persephone.... Stephanie...needed to be in place so that she could help make spring arrive for him.

He had big plans for the spring.

WHERE THE CHILD THINGS ARE

"Let me tell you something, kids: this is the house you two will raise your children in. It's perfect. And you're lucky, because it just came on the market and nobody else has seen it yet. You put your trust in Moffitt Realty, and we will take good care of you. That's a guarantee."

Alice looked up at her husband, unsure. She had always been uncomfortable with brassy types like Linda, but Paul had insisted on hiring her as their realtor. Linda had helped him sell his mother's old house last year, and she actually lived in this neighborhood herself. So, if Linda said it was a nice place to live, she must really mean it.

Paul wasn't looking at Alice. He was standing in the two-story entryway, gazing up at the chandelier above and the sweeping hardwood staircase. Alice had to admit that it really was a pretty house. And this one was much nicer than all the others they had seen at their price point. There were four bedrooms, three full baths, and a finished basement here. The previous owners hadn't even painted any of the walls an odd color like in that last house. Alice had wondered what on earth would possess someone to paint their whole house "tomato bisque?" The owners must have felt like they were living inside a pumpkin.

Paul reached out for her hand. "I think this is it, Alice. I have a good feeling about this place. What do you think?" He turned to her, his eyes bright. "We could start a family here. A fresh start. New life..." His bright eyes started to look wet now, as well as bright. He squeezed her hand and stepped toward the front bay windows to hide it.

Alice turned to Linda, who was already smiling like a Cheshire cat. "I guess we'll... make an offer?" The next fifteen minutes were taken up with signing papers again and again. Linda bustled off with her paperwork, dialing her cell phone as she strode toward her car with a "I'll text you as soon as I've presented the offer!" thrown over her shoulder.

"What do you say I take you out to dinner tonight and buy you a creme brûlée?" Paul was a changed man already. All the weight he had been carrying for the past few months seemed to be melting away, and Alice dared to feel a tiny flame of hope in her heart. She smiled up at her husband and nodded happily. He opened her car door for her, kissing her gently as she went past. Then, off to dinner they went.

It was hard for the couple to sleep that night, but luckily, the suspense didn't last long. Paul's phone, sitting on his nightstand, rang at 8:30 Saturday morning. Alice sat up and huddled up against his back as she tried to listen in.

"...Hey, Paulie boy! Who's your favorite realtor? C'mon...say it."

"Linda...you're killing me." Paul reached back and held Alice's hand tight.

"Kids, you've got yourselves a house! So, they're looking for a quick closing...something urgent with the family. Are you guys ok to move in within 3 weeks?" Linda spoke so loudly that Alice needn't have cuddled close; she could have heard the woman clearly from across the room.

"Yes!! Yes yes!! What's our next step??" Paul leaped out of the bed and started to rummage around in his nightstand for a pen and paper.

Alice smiled at his beaming face and got out of bed too, heading into the bathroom. She washed her face, brushed her teeth, and tried not to see all the boxes stacked in the closet nearby full of Paul's mother's belongings. *At least the new place will have enough space to store it all out of sight,* she thought, then immediately felt bad about it.

Alice shook her head to clear it of the unkind thoughts. Now that Selene had been gone for six months, and they had gotten their long-awaited check from the probate attorney, it was finally time to make a new start. Selene had never liked Alice, or at least, she had never liked that Alice had taken Paul's attention away from her constant drama. When she was alone, Alice allowed herself to smile at the fact that never again would a weekend getaway be cut short with a series of urgent phone calls demanding Paul come and help the workmen install the new washer and dryer or come assess what had gone wrong with Selene's computer. Their wine country weekend getaway had ended on Saturday afternoon when his mother had been absolutely positive that Russian twitter-bots had taken control of her laptop. That time, Alice luckily had been allowed to remain behind with the haul of their wine tastings. She was glad that Paul had never asked whatever happened to the bottle of Claret they had picked up at the dog-themed winery in the mountains. Alice had drunk the whole thing and hidden it deep in the recycling bin before he had come home, pleading a headache, and going to bed early.

They had been flat broke back then. Paul was a tax accountant for a huge firm in the city, but so far, he had only been given the smallest corporations to handle. His colleagues may have been assigned to law firms or hedge fund traders, but Paul was relegated to companies like A.S.M.O.D.E-US, which was just a property management company for planned neighborhoods. Paul tried so hard to make it a joke, saying "Oh, sure, maybe Dave handles the Mayor's office, but I'm the favorite accountant of the Association for Suburban Management & Organizational Development Enterprises, US branch! I'm a bigwig, babe!" He had worked more than 60 hours a week without a rise in salary for years, and he was starting to lose hope of any change. Inheriting Selene's estate was a welcome windfall, despite the circumstances.

"God, I hated her," Alice whispered to herself in the mirror, and then looked quickly toward the bedroom. Paul was still scribbling madly on his notepad. He was such a good man, but if Alice was truly honest with herself, she wasn't sure how much longer they would have lasted as a couple if his awful mother hadn't passed away. What had happened to her was a tragic accident: Selene had had a fatal interaction of her doctor-prescribed medication with a new vitamin supplement she had bought from some essential oil MLM scheme. She was sorry for Paul's grief, but Alice herself only felt the faintest hint of sorrow. Every time that they had gotten together with her, it was as if Alice could feel the weight of the woman's disapproval. Alice was not good enough for her son, and Selene had made it abundantly clear at every opportunity.

Paul finished the phone call and walked into the bathroom. He came up behind Alice and put his arms around her. "It's happening, babe. We're getting our own house." His eyes twinkled at her in the mirror, his chin resting on her shoulder.

She couldn't help smiling back at him. "I know." He nuzzled her neck and kissed her on the cheek, then started the shower to warm up.

Alice blew him a kiss and went down the hall to the kitchen of their tiny apartment to make coffee. *What would they do with all the space, three weeks from now?* In the apartment, it was a scant 6 steps to the kitchen from the bedroom. There were boxes in every corner and Selene's stuff crowded every closet and the entire space under their bed. What would it be like when it wasn't as if she was watching Alice's every move? When Alice could finally be the only woman in Paul's life?

The coffee finished brewing, and Alice poured some for herself and for Paul. He only liked a little cream in his, so she dribbled just enough to change its color before carrying it to him in the bathroom. He was just out of the shower and starting to shave. The prospect of the new beginning for both of them made everything seem rosier; they smiled at each other as they went about their own routines to get ready for the day.

When Paul had disappeared into the kitchen to make himself breakfast, Alice took a moment and pulled her packet of birth control pills out of the medicine cabinet. There were only 2 white pills left before the week of green pills. Maybe she wouldn't refill it this time. Just to see what happened.

* * *

Paul dropped the box he was carrying and turned to Alice suddenly, swooping her up into his arms. "Welcome home, madame. May I carry you over the threshold?"

Alice buried her face in his neck and giggled uncontrollably. "Oh my God, Paul. You're crazy." She pulled back and looked into his dear face. She kissed him, holding his cheeks between her hands. "Welcome home to you, too."

They walked hand in hand around the new house...THEIR new house. They toured the kitchen, opening and closing each cabinet and marveling at all the space for storage. They walked in tandem up the stairs and around the perimeter of each and every bedroom, leaving the master bedroom at the top of the stairs for last. Paul picked her up again and spun her in the middle of the room again and again. They spent a long time kissing, then walked slowly back toward the stairs.

"What's this?" Alice reached out her hand and touched the metal baby gate resting against the wall at the top of the staircase. The staircase down to the first floor had a solid wall along the entire right side but was open on the left. There were open wooden railings around the stairwell hole in the upstairs hall that u-turned at the newel post and lined the left side of the stairs going down. The gate Alice had noticed was mounted into the right-hand wall with sturdy hinges and could swing across the opening to the top of the stairs to latch securely at the newel post. It was exceedingly heavy, as if it were constructed of iron. "We don't need one of these for a while yet, don't you think?"

Paul shrugged. "Well, it swings back well out of the way. I don't see a reason to try and take it out, and maybe make an even bigger hole in the drywall than the anchors they must have used to install it. I think we should leave it for now. I mean...who knows what could happen?" He wiggled his eyebrows at her suggestively, and Alice giggled again and playfully slapped him on the arm.

They walked back downstairs together and started moving all their belongings from the car and rental trailer into their new home.

It felt so good, knowing that this was somewhere that SHE had never been, even though her inheritance money was what had made it possible. *It was the very least that old witch owed him, after all she did to us,* Alice thought as she carried a box of linens up the stairs. The box was heavy, and she paused at the top to catch her breath for a moment. Her leg brushed the baby gate, which made it rattle against the wall with a metallic clang.

Paul's voice rang up the stairs. "You ok, babe?"

"Yes...I'm fine," Alice called down. "I just bumped this gate up here. I'll be back down in a minute." She started to walk into the master bedroom, which faced the top of the stairs. For a moment, her leg was yanked backward, as if the cuff of her jeans had snagged on something. She quickly looked back, but her leg had already come free. The gate settled back against the wall with a small bounce and another clang. "Hm. I must have caught the latch", she murmured, and carried her box into the bedroom without another thought.

Moving into the house didn't take very long, since they really didn't have a lot of possessions. The basement proved to have ample storage for Paul's mother's memorabilia, so Alice found that the house really began to feel like THEIR home, not just Selene's storage area. It was a wonderful feeling, and it started to impact Alice in what she felt were very positive ways. She started experimenting with cooking new dishes in HER new large kitchen, she planted flowers out front that SHE chose without anyone telling her that flowers really weren't suited for that location. Even the HOA wasn't nearly as bad as Alice had always feared...they approved all her planting bed applications without any fuss at all.

One morning, Alice baked some cookies and worked up the courage to knock on the door of the house across the street. She hadn't seen much of the other neighbors, but this one seemed pretty innocuous: she was an older lady, probably a widow. Alice hadn't been close to her own mother, and after her disastrous mother-in-law experience, she was proud of herself for trying to make a new friend.

The door was opened by a short round woman with grey hair. Two cats twined around her ankles, eyeing Alice curiously. The woman nudged them back with her toe. "Psst Psst. Get back, you two. I don't feel like canvassing the neighborhood looking for you tonight. Can I help you, dearie?" She blinked up at Alice over her bifocals.

"Hi there, I'm Alice. I, uh, just moved in over there with my husband. I wanted to stop by and drop off some cookies and say hello. I haven't had a chance to meet many of the neighbors, what with unpacking and all." Alice realized she was babbling now, and quickly shut her mouth.

"Oh! Over at the old Pevensie place there? You're a tough cookie, you are. Do you want to come in? I can make some tea if you like. I hope you don't mind cats." She turned and started to shuffle away from the open door, shooing cats in front of her as she went and calling over her shoulder. "I'm Edith, by the way. Be sure to close the door behind you, dearie."

Alice stepped carefully in and used her backside to close the front door, as she was still holding the tray of cookies. She followed Edith through the house and tried to make small talk. "Oh, aren't your kitties cute! What are their names?"

"That fat one there is Lulabelle. The calico is Frodo, and the tuxedo cat up high is Alfred. There are a few more roaming around too. I just love my babies." Edith smiled at Frodo fondly, tickling him under the chin, then set about making tea. "So dearie, where are you from? Why did you move to Snowbridge?"

"Oh, we're originally from closer in toward the city, but Paul—that's my husband—his mother passed and left him some money, so we bought a house. It's a bit farther of a commute now, but we're thinking of starting a family, so—-"

"Well, like I said, dearie, you're a tough cookie. I'm not sure I would have the guts to move into that house if I was thinking of filling it with babies. But then again, it's none of my business... I don't like to pry, you know." Edith came to the table with two steaming cups of tea. She gestured for Alice to sit, and the younger woman obliged.

"The house? What's wrong with the house? It seems to be in very good shape. The previous owners took good care of— "

"Oh, sure they did, dearie. They were real nice folks, the Pevensies. They had a little boy; he was only a toddler when he— " Edith stopped talking suddenly and shook her head at herself. She reached out and took a cookie, washing her bite down with a sip of tea.

"When what?" Alice's voice came out much higher than usual.

Edith looked at her, then sighed. "As I told you dearie. I don't pry. But if you did some research at all you would find any number of news articles online on those interwebs, I'm sure." Edith set down her teacup and turned to face Alice squarely. "The Pevensie boy, Edmund... he disappeared. The police seemed to think he was murdered."

Alice gasped. "Oh my God! Linda didn't tell us anything about that! Isn't that a crime or something? I thought that realtors had to disclose that sort of thing."

Edith reached out and patted Alice's hand, which was still gripping her teacup with white knuckles. "Well,

I'm no lawyer, dearie, but I would bet that since the murder was never proven, and there were never any arrests, that it just counts as an odd disappearance. There's probably no legal requirement to report that. The boy could have been kidnapped or something, for all any of us know."

Alice looked down into her tea, her thoughts swirling. She should have known better than to try to reach out to neighbors; it would have been safer to just stay inside the house with her blissful ignorance. She tried to nod at Edith and stood up to leave. "I s-suppose you're right. Thank you for telling me, I guess. Uh...I think I have to head out now. I hope you like the cookies. Thank you for the tea. It was really nice to meet you."

She said this almost in one breath and she walked quickly toward Edith's front door. Just as she got to it and turned the knob, she felt a hand on her shoulder.

"I'm sorry if I upset you, dearie. I just figured if it were me, I'd want to know, you know? I wouldn't worry too much; sometimes bad things just happen to people, and you can't lose your head about it." She patted Alice's shoulder, let her walk out, then waved at her through the screen. "Come see me again soon, dearie. I like the company."

Alice waved vaguely at Edith and walked down the sidewalk. She pulled out her cellphone and dialed Paul. "Hey, you. Guess what? I just met one of our neighbors, and, boy, did she have a story to tell."

"Oh, really? Anything good?" Paul was audible, but just barely, over the din of the people talking in the background. Someday, they hoped, Paul would have an office of his own. For now, he was in a bullpen full of cubicles. He was easygoing enough that the noise day in and day out, and the constant parade of questions from clients, didn't seem to bother him. Alice, on the other hand, had to admit that his job was her own personal nightmare. Too much noise, too many people. Alice preferred to stay in her own little world.

"Well... anything good? No. Juicy gossip? Maybe. Somewhat terrifying? Definitely." Alice had drawn even with their house now. She paused to look at it a moment, then resolutely kept walking along the sidewalk, hoping some exercise would help as she passed along the news. "Edith—that's the lady across the street—I brought her some cookies and she told me all about how the old owners of our house either kidnapped or murdered their toddler."

"What?! No way. That's crazy."

"No, no, I know! It really is crazy! So, apparently the kid disappeared and there was never any arrest or anything, although a bunch of people thought he didn't actually go missing, but that one of the parents murdered him." Alice was walking faster and faster now, passing houses and driveways in a blur. "So, I guess it explains a little about how we got the quick closing and that they didn't argue with us on the lowball bid. Their 'family issue' was something pretty substantial."

Paul was quiet for a moment, but Alice knew the line was still connected from the jumble of voices still coming through the line. "We really should talk to Linda, don't you think? I mean, I thought stuff like that had to be reported to buyers."

"That's what I said too! But Edith said that maybe it wasn't required because there were never any charges filed."

"Babe, do you think that you could give her a call today? I know you have your article due soon, but they're really cracking down here on our call stats, and I need to get back to work. I don't want to get in trouble."

"No, that's ok. I can call her. Or...." Alice slowed down and stared at the woman locking the front door of the house nearby. "I could ask her myself right now. Call you later." With a quick, decisive movement, Alice ended the call, shoved her phone into her back pocket, and marched up the driveway toward her former realtor.

"Linda? I need to talk to you." Alice could feel the old knot in her chest at the idea of confrontation, but she had started out strong, so she tried to keep up the momentum. She placed her hands on her hips and tried to raise her chin and look directly into Linda's eyes.

"Hey, honey! How's the house doing for ya? Are you kids settled in yet?" Linda came up to Alice and wrapped her arms around her in what was obviously meant to be a welcoming hug. Alice didn't raise her arms to return it, and so they just stood awkwardly for a few seconds, Linda hugging Alice, and Alice standing rigidly with her hands trapped at her sides. Linda let go and stepped back. "Wow, honey. Is everything ok? You seem a little tense. Hey! I might have just the thing for that, you know. I am also a rep for this great company and we sell the most amazing essential oils and supplements— "

"Linda, we need to talk." Alice cut directly into Linda's new sales pitch. "I just met Edith Spade—she lives across the street from my house—and she told me all about the murder that happened there?" She crossed her arms and tried to give Linda a sharp look.

Linda rushed toward Alice, gesturing with her finger to her lips and glancing around. "Shhhh, honey. There's no need to shout things to the whole neighborhood. I admit, there was some...unpleasantness...surrounding the Pevensie family, but there was never anything proven. A lot of people were just convinced that it was a kidnapping by some random stranger. It was a tragedy, to be sure, but bad things happen all over, don't they? It sure isn't the house's fault." Linda smiled reassuringly, but Alice would have none of it.

"Why didn't you TELL us, though? My God, I feel like you lied to us just to make a quick sale!" Alice could feel her eyes filling with tears, but she blinked rapidly and fought them back.

"Oh honey, no. I would never do that! I care about all my clients. I live here in the neighborhood too; why would I shoot myself in the foot like that?" Linda tried to smile at her again, shrugging. "I mean, sure, legally I didn't have to report anything to you, and, according to the HOA bylaws I would actually be in major violation of the covenants for spreading gossip like that. It's just that Paul was so smitten with that house and you two looked so sweet together...I guess I just thought that maybe you two could bring some joy back to that place. That's all, I swear. I'm sorry if you're mad at me, honey, but I really thought you and Paul would be happy there."

Alice wasn't sure what to say, or do, to put Linda in her place, but she could tell that she wasn't going to get anywhere arguing right now. She settled for nodding at Linda primly and saying, "I guess...but you really should have told us." She turned and started to walk back home, then spun back and said what she had really been thinking. "That was a real dick move, though, Linda. And you know it." Astonished at her own daring, Alice turned and walked away as fast as she could. Linda didn't say a word as she disappeared down the street and around the corner.

Alice marched faster and faster along the streets, deep in her own thoughts. She waved politely back at a couple walking the other way on the sidewalk hand in hand and she was several feet past them when she realized they both had wooden Japanese-style swords strapped to their backs. She looked back over her shoulder, but they were gone.

Alice arrived back home, determinedly not looking across the street to where she was certain Edith was peering through the curtains. She unlocked her front door and went inside.

The door closing echoed oddly around the entryway; it sounded like the slamming of a door to a tomb. They really didn't have a lot of furniture or pictures or bric a brac or... anything. Alice and Paul had always lived in tiny apartments, and there was simply no room for them to have accumulated such things along the way. Maybe they could work on some new furniture or art or something...the echoes here would surely drive Alice mad after a while.

She decided to finish her article, then perhaps tackle unpacking some of the clothes upstairs. The deadlines had to come first now that there was a mortgage to pay. She made herself a snack and took it into the living room to work on her laptop from the comfort of the couch. Now was definitely the time to throw herself into her work so she didn't spend her time stewing about the possible crime scene that she and Paul had just bought with 10 percent down on a 30-year loan.

Her strategy worked, and a few hours went by as she put the finishing touches on her article. Alice wrote for a nationally-distributed digital magazine doing social commentary and cultural analysis...well...that was what she told people...and it was true, from a certain point of view. Alice had to admit that she would be glad if she never had to write another article with a title like: "Is your man a cheater? His glove compartment holds the answer," or "Which Jane Austen character are you?" Paul kept saying that her job was a stepping-stone to bigger things, and Alice hoped he was right.

Alice managed to send her finished article to her editor a full 2 hours before her deadline. She stood up and stretched, then carried her dishes into the kitchen. It was time to work on unpacking. She sighed to herself and walked past the bottom of the staircase, crouching to pick up a few stray pairs of shoes in the entryway before heading upstairs.

The gate at the top of the stairs was latched.

Alice stood up suddenly. That couldn't be true. She turned around and walked back to the foot of the stairs, her heart pounding.

Looking up the staircase, she could see now that the gate hadn't actually been fully latched to the newel post at the top. It was now swinging back to its normal resting place against the solid wall. It thumped gently against the plaster with a heavy metallic clank, once, then twice, then settled against the wall. The house fell silent again.

Alice couldn't breathe. It took two tries, but she managed to swallow, hard, then call up the stairs "H-Hello?" There was no sound in answer. She hoped that the silence was a good thing, as she was supposed to be alone in the house. She hadn't even thought about what she'd do if there was a reply.

Alice dropped the shoes, then bent and rummaged in another box in the entryway. She pulled out an old tennis racket and held it over her shoulder like a club, then slowly made her way up the stairs as silently as possible. She hoped her heart pounding wasn't as loud as it seemed to her in her ears.

She prowled around the bedrooms, checking in closets and under the bed, then returned to the top of the stairs. Alice carefully crouched and stared through the metal bars of the baby gate. Behind it, the eggshell-finish, beige-painted drywall showed through. It was all so normal looking. *I'm just being silly*, Alice thought. *Between Edith and Linda today, of course I would be completely on edge. I need to stop being such a scaredy-cat; it's starting to affect my sanity.* Alice squared her shoulders and marched into her bedroom, tossing the racket under the bed. Resolutely, she dumped a box of clothes out onto the bedspread and started to place them onto hangers. "Silly," she muttered to herself.

Inside the wall, something watched Alice though the gate's bars, and smiled.

* * *

Alice was having a terrible dream. Something was pressing on her chest, and she couldn't breathe. She tried to open her mouth to scream but was unable. Flailing with her arms, she tried to tear away whatever was holding her jaws shut. She sat bolt upright with the effort, and as she did, the pressure on her chest disappeared and she was finally able to open her mouth. She drew in huge gasping breaths, the sound loud in their nearly unfurnished bedroom. Her struggles had woken Paul, and he sat up as well.

"Babe? Are you ok? What's wrong?" He reached out and held her shoulders, which were still heaving with the effort of breathing.

Alice shook her head. "I—couldn't—breathe. Something—stopping—me. It—was—awful," she managed to say in between her gasps.

There was a loud metallic banging sound from the hallway, making both of them jump. It was too dark to see, so Paul carefully reached over and turned on his bedside lamp. Warm amber light flowed out their open bedroom door onto the newel post and the opening at the top of the stairs. Nothing was moving out there. Alice looked fearfully at Paul. He smiled and shrugged at her. "I'm sure it was just something shifting in one of the boxes downstairs. I'll just go look really quick." He got out of bed and slid his slippers onto his feet, then padded out the bedroom doorway and down the stairs. Alice gripped the covers in her fists tightly, waiting.

She could hear Paul shuffling around downstairs. There were no more noises, save for Alice's own tense breathing. After a few minutes, she could see his dim shape coming back up the stairs. When he got to the bedroom doorway, he stopped and shrugged at her. "Nothing is out of place. But that must have been it, that something just fell over in one of the boxes. It's funny though, how close that noise seemed to be." He climbed back into bed and put his arm around Alice's shoulders. "Come here, babe. I'll cuddle you up close and we can get some more sleep, ok?" He turned off his lamp, then wrapped his arms around her. He spooned behind her in the dark as they lay down facing the doorway.

It took a while, but eventually the sound of Paul's deep breathing combined with Alice's exhaustion overtook her. Her eyes drifted shut slowly, and just as she dropped off she could have sworn she heard a soft creaking noise and a metallic thump, as that of a door quietly closing. When morning came, she had forgotten the sound entirely.

Paul was already up and downstairs when Alice opened her eyes. She could hear him downstairs banging pots and pans and whistling off-key along the with music he was playing on the stereo. He was such a good man, despite his odd fondness for Nickelback. She smiled to herself and rolled onto her back, stretching luxuriously in the sheets. Why was it that sheets were always the perfect temperature when you wake up and then you don't want to leave them? Alice wiggled her toes in enjoyment, then flopped limply onto the mattress. Fine. She would get up...hopefully Paul had already made coffee. Alice swung her feet over the side of the mattress and shuffled into the bathroom to brush her teeth. Throwing a robe on, she walked out of the bedroom rubbing her still-bleary eyes.

Alice's foot caught on something at the top of the stairs, and she pitched forward. Her heart stopped as she flung her arms out to her sides, her hands scrabbling for something, anything to stop her fall. Her left hand caught one of the balusters on the railing framing the stairway, and then her right hand wrapped around the handrail on the opposite wall. She jerked to a stop, her body at an odd forward angle, feet still on the top step, her face suspended some four stairs lower.

Gasping, Alice slowly righted herself, gripping her hands tightly and stepping carefully down the steps until she could sit shakily on the stair. Her close call must not have made very much noise, as Alice could still hear Chad Kroeger singing downstairs about always waiting on a different story.

Alice remained sitting on her stair but turned her head around to look at the top step. "What on earth..." Alice muttered as she crawled up on her hands and knees, not quite trusting herself to walk upright yet. She reached out with a shaking hand and picked up a toy train. It was a decently-made one, with an engine and a caboose, plus four cargo cars in the middle. It was constructed of metal and heavy for its size.

Alice walked down the stairs slowly, holding the train in one hand and gripping the handrail tightly with the other. She walked into the kitchen and wordlessly held the train out to her husband.

"Hey babe...what have you got there?" Paul reached out and took the toy. "Hey...that's a pretty nice train. Is that something of ours? I don't think I've ever seen that before." He looked back at her quickly, his eyes lighting with an odd sort of hope. "Are—are you trying to tell me something? Is someone coming that will play with this train?" He rushed toward her, reaching out to hold her. Alice stepped back.

"Oh God, no! I mean...I'm sorry, Paul. I wasn't trying to tell you something coyly. I'm not pregnant. I tripped over that train at the top of the stairs just now. It could have killed me. I wondered if you had found something in an old box from your mom's house or something and accidentally left it at the top of the stairs."

Paul shook his head and looked back at the train. "Nope. I've never seen it before. It was at the top of the stairs, you said? I didn't unpack anything at all this morning...I just came straight down to make breakfast." He set the train on the counter, then came to Alice to rub her shoulders and look in her eyes. "I'm really glad you're ok, though. Would you prefer an omelet or sunny side up eggs? I'm cooking a big breakfast today." He kissed Alice on her nose and spun back to the stove to turn over the bacon.

Alice leaned on the counter and put her finger on the smokestack of the toy train's engine. She moved it back and forth slowly with her finger. It was such an odd thing to have found in such an odd place. She sighed. "Uh...whatever you're having, Paul."

"You got it. The coffee's already made. Do you want me to pour it for you, or do you want to do your creamer the way you actually like it?" He smiled over his shoulder at her giggle then set about cracking eggs into the frying pan in front of him.

Alice served herself a little coffee with a hefty slug of French Vanilla creamer and wandered toward the front of the house while Paul cooked. He seemed so happy here. Alice wished she could dispel the uneasy feeling she seemed to carry about all the time now. She stood in the entryway, looking out the glass storm door into the front yard, thinking.

Something laughed, off to her right. It was high-pitched, like a woman's or a child's laugh. She looked in the direction of the sound.

It had come from upstairs.

"Paul? Did you hear that?" Alice's own voice sounded strained and shaky, and far too quiet.

"What, honey? I can't hear you over the music." Paul was still rattling pans in the kitchen.

Alice couldn't answer, because at that moment, in front of her very eyes, the baby gate swung out toward the newel post all by itself. It didn't latch across the opening, instead, it reached the pinnacle of its arc, banging into the newel post, and came back toward its usual resting spot. Alice's ears couldn't hear the gate bump back into the wall over the music blaring from the kitchen, but she felt its impact in the pit of her stomach as if it were a punch.

The cup fell from her nerveless fingers with a crash, and the remnants of Alice's coffee went splattering around the tiled entryway along with the broken shards of her mug. A few of the splinters of glass went jabbing into the side of her foot, but she didn't react. Alice stood, transfixed, waiting for something else to move at the top of the stairs. She felt the blood began seeping out of her foot. Paul had heard the noise of the mug breaking and came running out to her.

"Babe, what happened? Are you ok? Did something startle you? Oh my God, your foot! I'll get you a towel. Did you get any glass in your foot? Honey? Babe? You ok?"

Alice could feel Paul patting her cheeks and trying to look into her face, but she was too busy watching the hand.

A hand had reached out from the wall behind the gate. It was tiny, and pink. The stubby fingers stretched out between the bars, then turned toward her, the fingers waggling in quick succession; a playful little wave meant just for her.

Alice screamed. She didn't stop screaming for a long time.

* * *

There was a beeping sound. Everything smelled weird. Antiseptic. The sheets were cold. Scratchy. Wrong.

Everything was wrong. Cold sheets were wrong. Tiny hands waving...waving...Paul and wanting babies and something beckoning to her from inside the walls. But there was bacon to be turned and cookies to be made and his mother...his mother...God I hated her, his mother. What is wrong with me? Did they give me something? Did Paul give me something? Did Selene finally get him to turn on me and give me something so I wouldn't be a good wife to him anymore? Why else would I start seeing things in the walls and babies and gates and babies waving, waving, and he was jealous I got to work at home because he had to be somewhere else in an office he hated and I could work in my pajamas but he wanted babies so here I am in this house watching the gate swinging, swinging, and it's swinging and the baby is waving at me and do I want to come see what's there... what's there? What IS there? Behind the gate? I'm Alice. I'm Alice, and I wonder. I wander. Alice needs to go through the looking glass but it isn't glass it's drywall, beige drywall, the most boring kind of drywall, but yet there was the pink hand and it's still waving but Paul wants little hands like that to play with trains that go Choo Choo Choo and back into the wall where it lives and I need to go see—-

Alice sat up. "I need to go see."

Paul jumped up from the chair he had been dozing in. "Alice, babe! Hi! Oh, you had me so worried!" He put his hands on her cheeks and held her face close to his, looking into her eyes. "I'm so happy you're awake. How are you feeling?"

Alice was in a hospital room. The beeping was coming from some sort of monitor somewhere down the hall. She had an IV in her hand and a bag of what looked like saline running in. There was a bouquet of sunflowers on the table nearby. Alice stopped looking around the room and focused on Paul. She reached out and touched his cheek in return.

"Hello. Paul, you look so tired."

Paul laughed ruefully. "Yeah, I bet I do. I've been sleeping in that chair for about 2 days now. It took the doctors a while to get the meds balanced out for you. You came here in the ambulance screaming your head off, and for a while everything they tried either had no effect or just knocked you out cold. They seem to feel pretty good about what they have you on now. Do you feel funny at all?"

Alice thought about that. "I'm not good at jokes. Why would a medicine make me funny?" Paul just stared at her. "Oh...Oh! You mean funny as in weird. Well, I would say, I don't feel quite like myself right now. But I don't feel like screaming anymore... or doing much of anything else anymore, either. I'm not sure I like it very much."

Paul nodded. "Ok, we will tell the doctor when he checks in on you." He paused awkwardly and scooted closer to Alice on the bed. "Babe? Can I...ask you something?" Alice nodded. "What happened the other day? If you start to feel agitated, we can stop. I just wanted to understand. You seemed fine, and then you just sort of...lost it. Did something scare you?"

Alice nodded again, unable to speak. Paul gestured to her encouragingly.

"I—I saw...something." Alice looked down at her hands resting in her lap, trying to find the words. "There's something wrong with that house, Paul. I've felt it since we moved in. I mean, all the weird sounds and things moving when they weren't supposed to and then that train...and the stories about the family that used to live there. I was already on edge. A-and then, the other day, while you were cooking, I heard something laughing at me. The sound came from upstairs. Then, something waved at me. It was like it wanted me to come in, but it was waving from the other side of the gate, behind the wall. IN the wall. It looked like a baby's hand..." Alice looked up at her husband her eyes wide. "My God, Paul! It was small...and p-pink...like a child's hand. D-do you think that it's that lost boy? The son of the previous owners?"

"Oh, honey, I really don't." Paul stroked her hair reassuringly. "I'm sure that you're just letting all the spooky stories get to you. You've been under so much pressure, what with Mom passing and us moving out here...and I think I've been adding to it getting all excited at the prospect of having a family of our own. But I want you to know," Paul added, holding her hands and looking in her eyes again. "There is no hurry at all for anything like that to happen. I just want us to be together, ok?"

Alice tried to smile back. "Ok," she said, with more assurance than she truly felt. But Paul wanted so badly for her to get better, so she needed to try, for his sake.

Over the next several days, Alice had to have interviews with a bunch of doctors about what she had seen and what had caused her "nervous breakdown." The general consensus between Paul and the doctors was that Alice had just snapped under the strain of so many big life changes at once. They all looked at her with the same air of patronizing indulgence, which Alice found aggravating. At first, she told the doctors the truth about seeing the gate move and the hand waving, just as she had told Paul. However, it soon became clear that sticking with this story was going to keep her locked up in a drafty hospital room with itchy sheets indefinitely. So, she started to play along with them when they hinted to her that it had been a hallucination of some kind. She had been asked several times whether things in the hospital room had moved around on their own, and she had said truthfully that they had not, which seemed to corroborate their idea of a temporary bout of insanity.

Finally, after almost a week in the hospital, Alice was discharged. The day was sunny, and Paul was being very sweet and solicitous, bustling about opening her car door and getting her buckled in to go home. As they drove, she stared out the window. The world seemed different: brighter somehow, and more colorful. Alice felt like an animal that had been trapped underground in the dark and suddenly released. She shifted in her seat, and her feet jostled her purse that had been set on the floorboard. It rattled oddly at the touch. There were no less than three different bottles of pills in there, and Alice was expected to keep faithful to her dosage schedule to prevent further "incidents."

Saddest of all, the doctor who signed Alice's release papers was very clear with her that while she was on the new medications, getting pregnant would be a very bad idea. Alice felt like she could hear Selene laughing at her in the back of her mind. She would have been glad that Alice was such a total disappointment as a wife. Now maybe Paul would have a convincing reason to leave her, like Selene had always hoped he would.

Alice gripped her hands into fists, her fingernails digging into her palms, as they crossed the bridge into the development. Paul navigated through the neighborhood and pulled into their driveway, leaping out of the car as soon as he had cut the engine and running around to open the passenger door. He took Alice's hand and escorted her to the front door. They walked into the entryway together, then stood awkwardly for a long moment, staring at each other.

Paul spoke first. "Well...what would you like to do?"

Alice hesitated, then decided. "You know what? I'd love to shower and rest in my own bed a little. Do you think I could do that? I could get cleaned up and feel human again, you know?"

Paul smiled. "Absolutely. Do you want me to draw you a bath? I could light some candles if you'd like." Alice patted his cheek and shook her head.

"No, Paul. Just a shower. I'll head up now, if that's ok?" She turned and walked to the bottom of the stairs. Her heart stopped a moment as she gazed up the staircase. She could feel Paul watching her.

Something was different. The stairway looked wider at the top...the gate was gone. Alice looked back at her husband, confused. He came and put his arm around her, looking up at the landing as well. "It was a suggestion from the doctor. It wasn't hard to take the hinges off the bracket up there, so I tackled that job yesterday. I figure, this way, we can have a nice fresh start in the house. Without the gate to remind you, it can be 'out of sight, out of mind,' right?" He smiled at her.

Alice nodded to him without speaking, then marched up the stairs, not sparing even a glance for the wall at the top where the gate had once rested. She strode into the master bedroom and shut the door, then went into the bathroom and shut that door too for good measure. She started the water in the shower to warm up, then sat on the edge of the soaking tub and shook all over. But she didn't cry.

Alice took her shower, combed out her wet hair (which finally smelled like her normal shampoo again and not the hospital kind), and put on her most fleecy pajamas. Now that she had gotten cleaned up, she didn't feel sleepy anymore. She decided she would go downstairs and see if she could help Paul with dinner; it would feel good to do something normal again. She reached out and turned the knob of the bedroom door, then stopped. She shook her head sharply at her own cowardice, then took a deep breath and pulled the door open. She stood for a full minute in the doorway overlooking the top of the stairs, waiting, and listening.

No sounds reached her. Maybe the doctors had been right, and she had hallucinated the whole thing. Alice walked down the stairs and into the kitchen where she found Paul sitting in the barstool at the counter, staring into space. He looked worried. She came up behind him and wrapped her arms around his torso, resting her chin on his shoulder. "How about some comfort food for dinner? Macaroni and cheese from the blue box? We could get all fancy and cut up hot dogs in it, if you'd like." She smiled at his profile, seeing him smile in return.

He stood up and turned to hug her. "You got it, babe. With extra ketchup?"

Alice giggled. "Is there any other way?" And so, they set to work, cooking and eating and talking about nothing at all. It was wonderful.

Night fell, and Alice took her last dose of medicines for the day. She was getting properly sleepy now, so she walked hand in hand up the stairs with Paul and let him tuck her into bed. He brushed his teeth and locked up the house, then climbed in beside her, spooning his body up to hers. Alice drifted off to sleep more easily than she had in a week.

Sometime in the dead of the night, Alice awoke with a start at an unexpected noise. It was an odd rhythmic thumping, slapping sound. It sounded like something being dragged across a picket fence, like in the old movies when little boys would run a stick along fences as they walked...finally, she placed the noise she was hearing. It was that of a hand being dragged along the spindles of the rail framing the stairwell along the upstairs hallway. Paul was still asleep, breathing steadily next to her on the bed. Alice was frozen in fear. The sound started at the other end of the hall, near the other bedrooms, then came closer to her door. *B-r-r-r-r-r-r-r-r-r-RUP!* Then it went back again. *B-R-R-R-r-r-r-r-r-r-rup.* Alice strained her eyes to see out the doorway to the landing, but was too dark to see anything moving. The sound came back toward the bedroom again. *B-r-r-r-r-r-r-r-r-r-r-RU—-*

Silence fell, and Alice rolled onto her back to listen. Then she felt a sudden pressure on her chest, and something covered her nose and mouth with an iron grip. Two glittering things came close to her face. Eyes. They were eyes, boring into her own. She tried to struggle but was weakening fast without any air. Her mind was racing, and her thoughts became clearer than they had been in a week.

They had never really understood the gate. When it was against the wall, that wasn't when it was open; that was when it was closed...it had been keeping something bound. No more gate meant that something now was free to come and go as it pleased. The thing sitting on her chest tilted its head this way and that as it considered her. She heard it laugh softly to itself, and she thought once more about the Pevensie child and what may have become of him. She felt its free hand stroking her hair as she lost consciousness.

* * *

Paul loaded the last box into the moving trailer, then he pulled the cord down to close the rolling door. He locked it with the padlock, then went back into the house for one last look.

He stood in the entryway, looking around at the house he had just moved into, yet was now leaving. He couldn't stay here; this place couldn't be a home if Alice wasn't here. He just wished he knew where she had gone. Over the past few weeks, he had realized that she must have blamed him for being committed to the psychiatric ward. But then again, she didn't remember the way she'd screamed that day. Paul had panicked and called 911 when his desperate attempts to reach her had failed. He desperately wished he could see her one last time, to apologize. Paul sighed to himself as he paced through the rooms, looking at spare bedrooms that had never been used for any guests, at the room he had dreamed of putting his first child to bed in, and, finally, at the room that he and Alice had briefly shared. It was time to go.

His steps were heavy with the grief he carried, so he rested against the newel post at the top of the stairs for a minute, then slowly trod down the staircase for the final time.

"Paul?"

His head whipped around. "Alice??? Alice, is that you?"

"Paul, can you come here for a minute? I want you to see something. Come up here, babe."

Her voice seemed to be coming from upstairs. *How could that be?* He had just been up there, and he had been all alone. He took a few shaky steps up, then paused. "Alice, babe, where are you? I can't see you."

Her voice sounded as if it was moving farther away now. "Paul, hurry. Come see. Please? I've missed you."

Paul walked up another half dozen steps, looking all around the upper hallway as he went. Still seeing no sign of her, he took the last two steps up to the upper landing. They were the last steps he ever took in this world.

Eventually, the house fell silent again, waiting.

HEART'S CONTENT

Kelly finished tying her blonde hair up into a ponytail and put on one more coat of lip gloss. She went into the closet to grab her running shoes, then trotted downstairs. Her kitchen was spotless as usual. She went into the refrigerator and poured herself a glass of her homemade strawberry and cucumber water, then checked her reflection in the mirror near the front door.

"Time to go, girl. We've got this." She smiled at her reflection in the mirror, then grabbed her keys and went out the door.

The "Moms on the Move" fitness group met every day after the morning bus drop, at 8:40 am on the dot. It was one of the few clubs officially sanctioned by the HOA, a fact that Kelly was inordinately proud of, even if the credit was undeserved. In truth, the HOA chair Lili had approached Kelly with the initial offer to start a group, saying that Kelly had been recommended by a mutual friend. Kelly had asked curiously which mutual friend they shared, but Lili's only reply was to smile and say "A very old friend."

Kelly, eager to have another feather in her cap, had let the matter drop and started recruiting followers. Some of the members would bring jogging strollers, but only the most elite of runners could match Kelly's pace while saddled with such a handicap. Kelly always reminded them: "You have to push yourselves, ladies! If you want to get your pre-baby body back, you can't be lazy; you have to chase it with all you've got! Taking care of yourself is the best way to be the kind of wife and mother your family deserves!"

"Heeeeey, lazy-ass!" Iris waved at Kelly from the playground bench. "Running late today, huh? It isn't often that I beat you here." Kelly smiled at her tightly and gave her a noncommittal shrug, barely stopping herself from rolling her eyes. Iris was one of those women whose entire personality seemed to be based upon being obnoxious: she had big, frizzy, box-dyed hair, thick brightly made-up lips, huge breasts, wide hips, and spoke so loudly that you could hear her clearly from the next block. She was tacky, she was crass, and she was proud of it. Kelly hated her viscerally.

"Maybe I didn't beat you to the meeting spot, honey, but you won't be able to keep up with me today. I am feeling on *fire*, girl!" Kelly smiled widely at Iris and tossed her shiny ponytail with confidence.

Iris snorted. "Oh, yeah? Well, most of us skip the amphetamines and just stick with coffee."

"Oh, Iris, you're such a c... a card," Kelly's smile had become less cheery, her voice much flatter than before. "It's like I was saying the other day, you really should start to sleep train Harley. The experts all say that any baby will learn to self-soothe; you just need to be firm and consistent. A well-rested mom has more tools to be her best, after all.

"I mean, it's what I've read about in all my research. Both of my kids slept through the night pretty much right away, but then again, I was SO fortunate to be able to stay at home and breastfeed them." She glanced down Iris' curvy body pointedly. "I mean, you have more than enough equipment, right?" Iris's eyes widened at the insinuation as Kelly continued. "I just don't know how you working moms do it. It must be just *torture* when you have a baby and then you have to give them to a stranger every day instead of doing your *real* job as a mother." Kelly blinked innocently, letting her words sink in, then tilted her head to the side at Iris in a pitying sort of way and clicked her tongue. "-tsk- You're so brave." She let her eyes glitter at Iris a calculated moment, then she turned her back and walked toward the new arrivals to the group.

"Good MORNING, ladies!" Kelly stood in front of the gathering new members, her hands on her narrow hips, her feet planted apart in an air of confidence. "I see some newbies here today. That's great, because I just loooove fresh meat!" She grinned broadly at the crowd. "Aw, I'm just messing with you...I'm totally a vegan. Now, as many of you know, I'm Kelly, and I'm the captain of Moms on the Move. We meet every weekday right here at 8:40 sharp. We stretch, then we leave at 8:45. Be on time, or be left behind. You don't want us talking about you behind your back, now do you?" Kelly winked conspiratorially, then continued. "Just kidding on that, too. Remember, we are all friends here. The aim of this group is to mutually support moms in this community to be the best they can be. It's a tough world out there on moms these days. This group here is a no-judgment zone, but at the same time, we don't accept any excuses. If you want results, you have to put in the work. Now, let's do some stretches really quick and then we'll be off. Today I'd love for us to get about 3 miles at full speed then we can let the stragglers go to a walk for the second loop. If you have a stroller, please keep to the rear of the group, ok? And for heavens' sake make sure your little ones are wearing hats and sunscreen!

I can't stand it when I see babies out in the sun without protection. Everybody ready? Let's go!"

Kelly led the group through some basic stretches for legs, calves, and some windmills to get blood flowing through their arms. Then she tightened her ponytail again and led the group out of the playground parking lot and down the paved walking paths that meandered all around Snowbridge.

Kelly loved leading the group through the neighborhood and waving at people out and about. One of the most fun parts of her morning was being sure to wave and call out to any of the moms who had either never come to—or had dropped out of—Moms on the Move. They always looked so sheepish when they returned her wave, and it gave Kelly a little thrill every time. She loved being the leader of something she could be proud of. As a blissfully happy, healthy, and successful mother and wife, she felt it was her mission to empower other women to take control of their lives too. Two babies and 7 years of marriage in, and she still could fit into her old size 2 daisy duke shorts from high school. She ran at least 6 miles a day, she cooked organic and vegan meals for her family every night, and her children had never tasted a soft drink in their lives, much less eaten anything close to processed food. She made her own laundry soap and scented it with essential oils bought from a local small business; that is to say, she was one of Linda's most loyal clients.

Half a mile in, Iris was already starting to fade. Kelly smirked to herself, but called back very loudly and encouragingly "Aw, come on, Iris! Where's all that motivation you had earlier?? Let's pick it up, now. Don't make it so easy on me." She heard Iris grumble under her breath and jog faster. "Attagirl, Iris! I knew you could do it!" She pretended not to notice Iris' raised middle finger in response.

146

The runners rounded the next cul-de-sac and had to come out into the street to avoid the driveway of Will and Ellie's house. The couple was standing on their driveway apron, laughing raucously. Near the doors to the garage was a large wooden target with several axes embedded into it. Ellie had a fistful of throwing knives in her hand and was ceremoniously handing one to Will, handle first. "Now, remember, my revenge on you will be swift and brutal. You made me laugh on my last throw. So for your turn, I shall be doing my impression of a drunk Scotsman on the tube who has mistaken an abandoned hairbrush for a hedgehog." Her eyes twinkled at him and she grinned wickedly.

The line of the running club arced out and around the end of their driveway, then back onto the sidewalk at the neighbor's apron. Every woman was straining to hear their conversation. The couple had become something of a favorite topic for the gossip mill of Snowbridge. They had moved into the neighborhood over a year ago, but they always seemed to be in their own little world. They were nice enough if you stopped to talk to them, but they never seemed to want to join in any community events or clubs. They could often be seen playing at sword fighting in the backyard, doing karate forms together, or, as they were doing now, throwing axes and knives. However, many of the moms secretly thought that the oddest part was that they seemed to be so goddamned *happy* all the time. Kelly, for her part, didn't trust anyone whose idea of marital bliss didn't include children.

The running group followed the sidewalk out of the cul-de-sac and headed to the halfway point of their run, near the entrance to the neighborhood. They looped the pond at the huge wooden "Snowbridge" sign, disturbing a few wandering ducks. Kelly gave a polite wave to Benny, who was out mowing the common area. He waved back, readjusting his earphones, and turned his mower to cut the next row. Kelly mused that it was rather early for Benny to be out mowing already; his hangover must not be as bad as usual. She called over her shoulder "Okay, ladies! We are now at the halfway point. This is your time to bail out if you can't hack it at this speed for the other half. If you choose to be a quitter, then I'll see you back at our normal spot tomorrow morning!" More than half the group peeled off at this point. Several dropped to a walk, but kept following Kelly's group, while the rest stopped entirely, flopping onto the grass nearby or crouching over their knees to catch their breath.

"Bye-eeee!!" Kelly waved again and charged back into the heart of the neighborhood, women and strollers trailing in her wake.

* * *

After a shower and a quick cleaning of the house, it was time for Kelly's daily devotional time. Her main floor was full of carefully chosen cottage-style art and inspirational quote prints. She strode past a primitive "Live / Laugh / Love" sign and a "Happiness is Homemade" sampler, then hurried down the steps into the unfinished basement. She shimmied behind the neatly stacked and labeled Christmas decorations in their color-coordinated red and green bins and she knelt down on the cold cement at her altar. She lit the black candles and threw a pinch of brimstone powder into the censer.

"O Great Kog'druran, I honor thee. I am thy humble servant, that thou mayest also bestow upon me thy bounteous blessings. I am ready to receive your instructions, should you require my service on this day." Kelly bent low to the ground, her hands stretched before her, palms up. She came here each day to pray to her patron demon. Most days, it was a very short session of praying, praising, waiting, and then moving on with her day. But after pledging your blood oath to Kog'druran you did not lapse in your duties. Not even once.

She waited, the rough cement digging into her knees as it always did. I really should put a rug down here, she thought, but it might attract attention from Brendan or one of the kids. On the other hand, she didn't need the Moms on the Move group to comment on the state of her knees. That would be just up Iris's alley to—

Her train of thought was interrupted by a concussive feeling and a bit of brimstone smoke. It was like being near a cannon blast—like a punch to the chest—but there was no noise whatsoever.

"Hey, Kelly! What's shakin', bacon?" Kog'druran was a relatively young demon, as far as Kelly could tell. But he had definite power behind him, and she saw no reason why an up-and-coming patron demon was a bad thing. He could take her with him as he rose (or would it be fell?) in the ranks of his kind. The only drawback was, he seemed to have really enjoyed his time leading a large Satanic cult back in the 1970's, and his speech patterns had never really recovered.

"Greetings, mighty master. I am honored to be in your presence once again. May I ask, do you have need of me on this day? I humbly await your command." Kelly looked up briefly as she said this, not quite meeting the demon's glowing yellow eyes, then prostrated herself once again.

"Uh, yeah, babe. Look, I've been very generous to you, haven't I? I mean, you are a really lucky chick: two cute rug rats, a nice house, a rocking bod... so, I've been thinking... " The demon crossed its four arms and leaned back against the stack of plastic storage boxes, his horns scraping them gently as he looked up at the underside of the floorboards above in contemplation.

"Of course, my master. I am indeed blessed to be in your service and receive the many gifts you have bestowed upon me." Kelly didn't look up this time, but she spoke very rapidly in the hopes that he would get to the point so she could get off her knees. She wished she had stretched a bit more this morning; her leg muscles were really complaining.

"In order to start repaying me, you will need to start, uh, filling my bank, if you feel me. Either you need to recruit some more followers for me—which would mean that you would then be in competition with other humans for my favor—or... " Here the demon smiled, his rows of sharp teeth gleaming in the candlelight. "...I will require another sacrifice. I mean, babe, how long has it been since the last one? A few centuries or something?"

"Uh...it has been a while, my master." Kelly hedged, as her insides twisted at the thought of another sacrifice. The last one had been a while ago, but not, of course, centuries. It had been almost twenty years since Kelly had first proved her dedication to her master, and it had been awful. She had really loved that dog.

"I thought so." The demon tapped his head with a taloned finger. "I remember everything, little mama. But this one has to be bigger. More... groovy. You dig?"

"Bigger, my master?" Kelly felt a bead of sweat run down the center of her back, sending a cold shiver in its wake.

"Let's just say, I've lost my taste for the lesser creatures of your stupid little realm. I want a human this time."

"A—are you certain, master? If anyone should find out what I have done, I will be imprisoned and then I can't be in your service anymore. I could more easily cover up something a little less— "

Kog'druran interrupted her with a snarl, and he put a taloned finger under her chin and raised her head to look at him. "Do you doubt my power?" he growled, his voice low and dangerous.

"No! Of course not, master. I was just afraid…"

"Aw, chill out there, mama. I've got your back. You give me what I need, and you will be taken care of and rewarded." He leaned down close, transfixing her with his yellow eyes. "Fail me… and you will be very sorry."

"Y—yes, master. I won't fail you." Kelly bowed again, shaking.

"I thought so. Then, until next time, babe. Catch you later!" The concussive force again, a puff of brimstone smoke, and he was gone.

Kelly sat up and hugged her knees to her chest. Another sacrifice…but from where? And a human, this time? Where on earth would she find someone who wouldn't be missed? Nobody was that annoying, except maybe— Kelly gasped as inspiration struck. She could kill two birds with one stone: appease Kog'druran AND rid herself of her least favorite person, ever. She smiled at the idea. This one would be almost fun, if not for all the mess to clean up afterward.

Kelly blew out the candles and went upstairs. It would be worth it in the end, she knew that. After her first sacrifice, her teenage skin had cleared up overnight and her previously flat chest had filled out nicely. Boys had taken notice, and eventually, the homecoming queen's crown was on her head. Life had been very pleasant for Kelly since then, and she owed it all to the smart decision to acquire a patron demon. After all, she just wanted what she deserved: to continue living her best life. Kelly paced restlessly in her living room, trying to think of a plan. An idea came to her, as they always did, so she pulled out her pink cell phone and dialed Iris' number.

"Iris? Hey, girl! How are you doing? Feeling ok after the run this morning? Haha! No, I'm just kidding, girl. Don't be so sensitive. You were looking great out there today. No, really, I mean it!" Kelly rolled her eyes to herself in the hallway mirror, then turned to check out her rear end in the reflection as she continued. "So... I was wondering...are you busy after running club tomorrow? I was wondering if I could offer you coffee or tea or...maybe a mimosa? You know I'm famous for my special recipe... yeah? Great! So, can you head over to my place right after you clean up a bit? I mean, I know I always like to freshen up after running...right! Haha! Ok girl, I'll see you tomorrow morning. Bye-eeee!" Kelly ended the call and put down her phone. She needed to do a bunch of tasks in preparation for tomorrow's work: purify the sacrificial blade, scrub herself down with salt, remember where she had stashed the hypodermic needles...oh, and bake 36 cupcakes for the bake sale tomorrow. "No rest for the wicked," Kelly said out loud wryly, then winked at herself in the mirror before striding toward the kitchen to get started. Tomorrow was going to be a busy day.

* * *

Kelly got up extra early the next morning and made a big pancake breakfast for everyone. Brendan and the kids happily scarfed down vegan "chocolate" chip pancakes, then the children came dutifully to their mother to have their sticky faces wiped before heading out to the bus stop. Brendan gave his wife a kiss and a pat on the backside, then left for work. Kelly quickly loaded the dishwasher before hurrying out the door herself to meet the running club.

Although it killed her to do it, Kelly slowed her pace enough that morning so that Iris could easily keep up and even shouted encouragement to her a few times without the slightest hint of audible derision. The group rounded the neighborhood entrance, and two moms that had lagged back with the walkers yesterday stayed with the main running group. Kelly led everyone in a cheer for the two women, then took the group around the sidewalk loop past Will and Ellie's house. They were doing something sedate for a change, sitting on their porch with cups of coffee. "Lazy day today?" Kelly said to them brightly as she waved.

Ellie smiled back and raised her cup in salute. "Late night last night. Did you get to see the meteor shower? It was fantastic." She turned and smiled at Will, reaching for his waiting hand. He toasted his coffee to her and winked broadly.

"Aw, no I didn't! Darn it! Ok then, see you later...Bye-eeee!" Kelly called over her shoulder as they passed back up the street. "Meteor shower?" she murmured questioningly to the woman closest behind, receiving only a vague shrug in return.

After running club was finished for the day, Kelly checked in with Iris to be sure she was still coming by later. "How long do you need?" she asked, looking Iris up and down appraisingly. "I can be ready in less than half an hour, but if YOU need more time...."

Iris smirked at her. "Nah, I'm like a speed demon. I'll be there in about 30, no problem." She turned and walked off to her car. It had always vaguely irritated Kelly that Iris drove her car for just a few blocks each morning just to meet the running club, rather than get the smallest amount of extra exercise. Annoyance giving her a burst of energy, Kelly jogged the entire way back to her own house, unlocked her door, and started to set out her sacrificial instruments. She had the anointing oil, the knife, a chalice to catch the blood, and the assorted cleaning supplies for after the job was done, including a large plastic storage tub for the pieces left over.

She carried them all downstairs and arranged everything near the altar, then dashed upstairs to shower. Kelly was just pouring the champagne into flute glasses when the doorbell rang. "Come iiiiiiin!" she sang out. "Door's open!"

"Hey there...damn, it's clean in here...do I need to take my shoes off or something?" Iris called out from the entryway.

"Not at all, silly! You're a guest! Now, get in here and let me know if you want more or less Chambord in this; basically, do you prefer 'baby pink', or 'shark attack'?" Kelly laughed merrily at her own joke.

"Uh, whatever you're having is fine." Iris rounded the corner into the kitchen. She sat herself on one of the farmhouse-style barstools. "So, I'm not exactly sure why you invited me over here today, I mean, we've never been what I'd call 'friends', but I do love mimosas and I had the day free, so... " Her words petered out and she drummed her long acrylic fingernails on the counter awkwardly.

"Oh! Well, I guess I had two reasons." Kelly said, pouring Chambord into the glasses and making sure to swirl it around so the sleeping powder in Iris' glass would dissolve better. She hoped that Chambord's cloying sweetness would mask the bitter taste of the powder. "First, I came across a whole bunch of Maximillian's old baby clothes and they're like new. I was wondering if you'd like any for Harley before I drop the rest of it off at Meadowbranch Hospice for a donation." She turned around from where she had been mixing the drinks, a glass held in each hand. "And second, I feel like we never really get to talk, you know? And I believe that the more mom friends you can make, the better off you are. Nobody really understands the struggles we moms face except us, don't you think?" Kelly held out Iris' glass to her with a look that expected agreement.

Iris accepted the offered glass and took several long swallows, then smacked her lips and burped. Kelly's eyelid twitched, but she managed to smile indulgently at the other woman and shrug off the rude noise. She turned, picked up the champagne bottle, and topped off Iris's glass. "Cheers!" Kelly sipped her own drink, then leaned across the counter toward Iris. "So, did you want to come and take a look at the baby clothes? I'm sorry, but I'm going to have to ask you to come with me to the basement to look. It's, like, a *huge* box and it would take two people to carry it. I would have asked Brendan, but he had to leave SO early for work today. He's got such an important and demanding job, as you know. Anyway...shall we?" Kelly gestured toward the basement door.

Iris quickly downed the rest of her second glass of champagne, then set it down on the counter. She stood up from her stool with marked effort. Kelly's smile grew wider, and she went to open the basement door. She waited as Iris tottered to the top of the stairs. Iris paused and looked at Kelly oddly, almost with a hint of uncertainty. Kelly raised her eyebrows and smiled again. "The box is just to the left as you get to the bottom of the stairs. After you, girl!"

She gave Iris a few stairs' distance before surreptitiously pulling the hypodermic needle out of her pocket. Iris reached the bottom of the steps and turned as she had been directed, and it was at that moment Kelly rushed at her. Iris had about 4 inches of height and at least 60 pounds on Kelly, but the smaller woman leapt at her from a few stairs' up, wrapping one arm around her neck and pulling Iris' head to the side. With her other hand, Kelly jammed the needle into the woman's neck and pushed the plunger. They both fell to the cement floor with a resounding crash, banging Kelly's elbow on the concrete in the process. Her eyes stinging with tears from the pain, she nevertheless held tight as Iris thrashed about. Her head connected painfully with Kelly's, making her see stars. Kelly counted slowly to 100 as Iris's struggling dwindled until she lay still. It was only then that Kelly started to extricate herself from the other woman. "Cheese and crackers, Iris, I don't think our running club has been doing you much good in the weight loss department. You should have tried that juice cleanse we all did last month, at the very least." Kelly stood up, smoothed her ponytail and straightened her clothes, then winced as her bruised elbow complained about the motion.

"Now, let's get started, Iris. First things first, I'm going to put on these coveralls because I really don't want your stinky blood all over me. Then I'm going to have to drag you over here to the altar and anoint you with the ritual oils. Hopefully my master will be able to tell I've done this part, because I can barely smell them over that god-awful cologne you've been bathing in. Didn't I give you time to shower? I wanted a lovely sacrifice for my master and here you are ruining it." Kelly nudged the Iris' prone body hard with her toe, then, sighing, bent and dragged her by the shoulders of her jacket to in front of the altar. Kelly lit the candles and sprinkled the brimstone around, then, dabbing the oils on her own head as well as Iris', she took up the sacrificial dagger.

The ritual was very simple, but there was no room for error, either. Once the actual sacrifice was done, there was the blood to be drained into the chalice, then a quick dismembering so that she could store the body for Kog'druran to help dispose of it.

What if he doesn't help? Kelly decided she had no time for intrusive thoughts. She shook her head at the notion, cleared her throat, and started the last phase of the ritual.

There was one silver lining to all the trouble of the morning: the combined effect of the drugs meant that Iris didn't suffer—or, at least, she didn't react—when Kelly made the first cuts to drain her heart's blood into the ceremonial chalice as an offering to Kog'druran. By the time she finished arranging Iris's entrails into the proper sigils, Kelly was sweating with the effort. Kelly bitterly resented the fact that she hadn't perspired like this during this morning's run, and perhaps that was why she took a few liberties during the dismemberment. Iris should have been able to run like a gazelle with thigh muscles like these, Kelly thought as she struggled to free Iris' left leg from its socket with her knife. Finally, it came free.

"Hey, Iris!" Kelly panted a little as she swung the leg over her shoulder like a lumberjack, Iris' sneaker-clad foot dangling over her shoulder. "Check this out, girrrrrrrrl! It didn't work when I tried, so maybe you'll finally listen when you KICK YOUR OWN ASS!" Kelly swung the pink shoe several times into Iris' backside, then clubbed her in the head a few times for good measure. Her anger spent, she lobbed the leg into the plastic bin nearby, where it landed with a wet thud, the bin skidding a few inches away.

"You tripping, baby? You gotta chill out there, mama. A sacrifice is a serious occasion, you know." During her little tirade, Kelly hadn't felt the usual concussion that signaled his arrival. She spun around in shock and surprise. Kog'druran was standing at the altar, his hoofed feet straddling what was left of Iris. "Of course, if this was a true sacrifice…that would have been a problem." He reached down and picked up the chalice full of blood, taking a measured sip. Then he made a face and spit it back out. "What in the Seven Hells is this swill? Did this human exist solely on fried food?" He tossed the chalice carelessly to the floor, the blood spilling out onto the concrete. Kelly fell to her knees and prostrated before the demon.

"Oh, great master, what have I done wrong? I anointed the sacrifice, I made the sigils, I drained her so that you might drink…why are you displeased? Please, I beg you, tell me so that I may correct the wrong I have done." Her hands were spread flat on the floor, and she could feel the creeping puddle of blood from the chalice wetting her fingertips, but she didn't budge.

Kelly could see his hooves step directly in front of her face where her nose was nearly touching the ground. She shook in anticipation. "This. Is. Not. A. Sacrifice." His voice was low and dangerous, barely above a whisper, but she could feel it rumble in her very bones. "You humans... you can't just kill any old thing and call it a sacrifice. You have phones in your pockets now that can access the depth of human knowledge, yet you don't understand such a simple thing?" He crouched and tapped her on the top of the head with his long talon. She looked up at his face, terrified. He smiled a dangerous smile. "A sacrifice must be something that you love. Something that you will miss. Something that is an ACTUAL FUCKING SACRIFICE!" He yelled these last words into her face, his breath smelling of brimstone and blood and rot.

Kelly cowered before him again. "Y-yes, my master. I am sorry. B-b-but...what can be done about...." She didn't dare to raise her head, but gestured with one bloodstained hand vaguely toward the carnage on the basement floor.

Kog'druran stood again and started walking back to the altar. "My protection is only granted to my loyal minions who have paid proper tribute. Perhaps if you were one of those again, I might be able to help you clean up this mess you've made. But I would have to be appeased, first. After that, I'll decide." There was the concussion without sound again, and he was gone.

Kelly slowly sat up and regarded the mess around her. She sat there for several minutes, unblinking, with her eyes pouring tears down her sweaty and blood-spattered cheeks. Then she made a sharp sound deep in her throat, retied her now-dusty blonde hair into a tight ponytail once more, and began to scrub.

She almost didn't finish in time. The body parts were already in plastic bins, so they got unceremoniously shoved into the corner of the storage area to wait for her master's future help. The last garbage bag full of bloody cleaning rags was just being tied up and dropped into the bin outside as the children were walking home from the bus stop. Kelly plastered a smile on her face and marched into the kitchen. Brendan would be home soon, and he would expect dinner on the table as usual.

The usual evening routines of dinner, then homework, then baths and bedtime followed. The kids were tucked in for the night and Brendan had already climbed into bed with his novel. Kelly pleaded exhaustion and pretended to go to sleep early. She waited, perfectly still, until she heard the antique mantel clock chime 3 am. Then, she slid the hidden knife out from between the mattress and box spring on the side of her bed and crept, cat-like, into the hall. She stood for a long time in the upstairs hallway, still trying to make her decision. There were three bedrooms to choose from.

A sacrifice. Something you love.

Finally, she turned and headed toward the room she had chosen, her knife clutched tightly in her fist. She only hoped that this offering was enough to satisfy him.

SATAN'S LITTLE HELPER

From the journal of Katie Jones, age 7:

11/30

    I am very excited today because tomorrow our Shelf Elf will come! Mom says he works for Santa Claus the rest of the year, but at Christmas time the elf comes and stays with us to make sure we are good and get lots of presents. I kind of think it's weird that this elf has to report to Santa. I thought he just knew if we were bad or good, like they say in the song. My friend Jenny says their elf last year did all sorts of silly things every day, so maybe it will be cool. I hope he sees how good I'm going to be, because I want Santa to bring me something extra special this year. I want him to make my parents stop fighting.

12/1

    Our elf came this morning! When I went to the kitchen to have my cereal, he was sitting in my special dinosaur bowl! He had a little sticker on him that said "Hi, my name is Sully and I'm your new Shelf Elf!" My mom thought I wasn't happy to meet him, but I think I was just surprised. I expected him to look different, I guess. He doesn't look like the ones I've seen in the stores. His face is more real-looking than those, and his eyes are red. Mom says they're brown, but I think they're red. I also wanted to know why Mom said that Santa dropped the elf off to watch us, but if that's how it works, how is it you can just buy them in the store too? Are those ones not alive yet or something? My mom says not to ask too many questions and it's just part of the magic of Christmas. I think she just didn't want to answer me.

12/4

Okay, maybe this elf thing is kind of cool after all. This morning, when I went into the bathroom to brush my teeth, Sully the elf was fishing....in the toilet! There were some of those gummy Swedish fish floating around in there. It was so funny! I was really glad it wasn't anything gross in the toilet, though. It was too bad that mom said there weren't any non-toilet Swedish fish left for me to eat.

Dad thought the fishing thing was super funny too. Mom said "Of course you would think so" in a weird way, and Daddy made a mean face back at her. I don't know why he did that.

12/6

Today the elf did the funniest thing! He tied up all my Barbies and hung them from my ceiling fan pull chains! It took me forever to put my shoelaces back into my shoes, though. I almost missed the bus. My mom asked me why my Barbie dolls all had to be naked, and she didn't believe me when I told her I didn't put them away like that. Daddy wouldn't stop laughing, and Mom said he was being "in a pope writ" ...whatever that means.

12/7

This morning was so crazy. When I woke up, the elf was sitting on my nightstand holding a marker, which was super weird. But when I went to go brush my teeth, I saw that he had drawn ALL OVER MY FACE! I had whiskers and dark eyebrows and a mustache! And then... you won't believe this... I went to go tell Mom and Daddy about it and they were both in the bathroom scrubbing marker off their faces too! I laughed and laughed, but Mom and Daddy didn't seem happy. Mom kept asking Daddy why he had done it, and Daddy kept saying that it must have been the elf. She threw her washcloth at him, and he caught it and threw it back in her face, hard. I felt kind of scared then, but Daddy told me that it was ok; Mom just needed to learn to treat him with respect. I guess that's right because they're always talking about respecting people at school.

It took me a long time to get the marker off my face, but I am glad that Sully didn't use the permanent markers, because that would have been even worse to clean off.

12/10

I didn't think the elf would do anything new today. When I was in bed last night, I got thirsty and went to go ask for a drink of water. I caught Mom putting the elf in her dresser drawer... I thought maybe she was just tired of his messes and wanted him to stay put for a night. But then, this morning, I woke up early because I could hear Mom running all around the house. She was opening drawers and cabinets and checking in the washer and dryer. I asked her what she was looking for, because I thought maybe Sully had escaped from her drawer.

Well, it turns out that he did, because she wasn't looking for Sully at all; she had been looking for all of her underwear and bras! She said that her drawers were empty this morning when she tried to get dressed.

I was the one who found them for her. Sully had taken all of Mom's stuff and HUNG IT IN THE TREE in the front yard! He was sitting on the mulch leaning against the trunk with his arms crossed like he was waiting for us to find him.

Mom got the stepladder and a pair of long grill tongs and got all of her stuff out of the tree. Daddy didn't help her at all; he just stood on the porch watching and making weird jokes about getting in trouble with the "Haitcho Way." Like, if she didn't hurry the Haitcho Way police would come and take her to jail or something. Mom took all her stuff inside and then locked herself in the bedroom for a while. I'm glad that I didn't have to go to school today or we would have been SO late. Haha!

12/16

Today when I got home from school, I found out that Sully the elf did something super naughty. He spilled flour all over the kitchen table and did snow angels in it. I tried to clean it up so Mom wouldn't be mad at having to clean up the mess, but I spilled flour on the floor and then I had to go looking for the dustpan. Daddy wanted to know why I needed cleaning stuff, and so I had to show him what Sully had done. He rolled his eyes and said "I told her I wasn't doing it so now she's just making extra work for me with this stupid elf?" Then he said some cuss words I'm not allowed to say (or even write in journals).

I don't know what he was talking about, though. I thought Sully was *supposed* to do pranks.

We cleaned everything up together and I put Sully up on the bookshelf to watch us, so he could make sure to see that I was being good and helping Daddy to clean up.

12/19

I woke up early today because there was a lot of yelling. I sneaked down the hall to Mom and Daddy's room and he was very mad. I saw that there was a huge shaved spot in the side of his hair. He was holding Sully in his fist and waving it at Mom. He said she had gone too far this time, and what was he supposed to do at for work today because he had a big meeting to go to. Mom didn't even get to answer him before he hit her in the face. She didn't cry like she usually does when that happens, though. She just stared at him. I must have stood there too long, though, because then they saw me, and I was in for it because they both decided that I must have been the one who shaved Daddy's head.

I kept telling them I didn't do it and it must have been the elf. I wouldn't want to do something naughty because I wanted presents from Santa. They didn't believe me, though. I got a spanking from Daddy AND I got my tv time for the next week taken away by Mom, even though I didn't do anything wrong. It's not fair! And even worse, I saw Daddy throw the elf in the trash can outside. I don't think Santa is going to be happy about that at all.

12/23

Daddy wasn't home when I got up this morning. I overheard Mom talking on the phone to Grandma, and she was saying things like "at least he didn't take Katie when he left," which I didn't understand. Why would I want to go to work with Daddy? His job is boooooorrring. But then Mom kept asking me whether I had seen Daddy or if he had said anything strange to me last night, so I guess maybe he didn't go to work today after all. Mom seemed scared, but I'm not sure why. Daddy even left the car behind for us to use today. That was really nice of him, wasn't it?

And, do you know the weirdest thing of all? Sully was sitting in my Christmas stocking this morning. I don't know how he got out of the trash can, but now Santa will be able to take Sully home to the North Pole tonight after all. I don't even care about what he's going to leave under the tree, because he's already given me the present I wanted most.

Mom and Daddy aren't going to fight again, because I'm pretty sure Sully took Daddy away somewhere he can't hurt us anymore.

I love Sully. I hope he comes back next year.

EPILOGUE: ALL'S HELL THAT ENDS HELL

The HOA meeting that month was tense. Lili, as head of the HOA Management Company, called the meeting of "A.S.M.O.D.E.-US / Snowbridge" to order. Almost immediately, hands were in the air asking to be recognized. The complaints were numerous, varied, and absolutely bizarre:

- "I don't think the running club should be sponsored by the HOA. Personally, I feel like it gives preferential treatment to certain families."
- "I think my neighbors are aliens."
- "Can we put up a sign saying the playground isn't a skateboard park?"
- "That guy with the super nice lawn is totally creepy and there is a weird smell coming from his yard."
- "The family across the street has something living in their garbage cans. It woke me up the other night as it rummaged around in there. Something has to be done."
- "Can't any of the realtors in town do something about that terminally-vacant house next door? It keeps selling for lower and lower prices... it's wrecking my property value!"

‾ "YOUR property value?? What about me? The chick next door to ME was loaded into an ambulance last week all bloodied up and I think she was handcuffed to the stretcher!!"

Lili pounded her gavel on the desk. "Ladies and gentlemen!! Please! Thank you for all your input, but before we get to new business, we must follow what has already been put on the agenda. Now, my colleagues and I have been regularly meeting this past month, and we have come up with some very exciting new statutes that we all need to vote on. Can everyone please pay attention here? Eyes on me, please? All right, then, we can begin. Erik? Can you lock the exit doors please?" The assembled homeowners didn't react to this last odd request, as they were all transfixed by the glowing gemstone held up in Lili's hand. Erik, her assistant, started locking the exit doors around the meeting hall one at a time.

Lili's eyes began to glow red, shining even brighter than the gem she held. "You are all very fortunate, as you will soon serve a much greater purpose than most in this community. You will be my slaves, my emissaries, that will journey outward and bring more recruits into our fold. You, my disciples, will help grow Snowbridge even larger than before, and bring power and glory to my name! Soon all will bow befor— "

The side door of the meeting room burst open, and Erik jumped back; he had just been walking over to lock that one. Will and Ellie tumbled in one after the other, both a bit out of breath.

Ellie smiled around the room at everyone, even though only the HOA's officers had the free will to look back at her. They did not smile in return. She shrugged. "Hell-LO, you guys," she said brightly. Will and I were just thinking... maybe it's time for a change of management around here." She reached over her shoulder and drew a katana from the sheath on her back. She grinned sunnily over at Will, who was now standing in a semi-crouch beside her. He smiled back and winked. In his hands were a machete and a trench knife, freshly drawn from his multi-pocketed tactical pants.

The board of the Snowbridge Homeowner's Association drew together in a group facing them. Lili still held the glowing gem in her hand. The other residents of the neighborhood stayed in their places, as much a part of the scenery as the motivational posters lining the walls.

One by one, the board members changed into their true forms. Erik became a slavering demon with blue skin, pointed fangs, and horns. The vice president, Chris, had ragged wings and a club foot. Behind her was Sam, who had transformed into a hook-nosed and mucus-covered monstrosity. Still another member, Thomas, had turned into a hairy beast whose smell quickly permeated the room.

In front of them, Lili stood in all her glory. She had grown feet taller, her arms and legs now thin and spidery looking. Her eyes still glowed red, and her hair waved behind her in a nonexistent wind. She, too, had wings, but unlike Chris' ragged, feathered ones, hers were draconic, with sharp talon-like points on the tips. They reached even above her head and dragged along the floor behind her. She flexed her hands and screamed at them like a banshee, her mouth dropping open inhumanly wide.

An uneasy silence fell as each side waited for the other to make the first move. Suddenly there was a quick knock at the door nearest Will and Ellie. The fire escape creaked open, and Brian's head poked around the door. "Uh, hi there you guys." He came into the room and let the door slam behind him, the sound abnormally loudly in the silence of the rec center. "So, Will, uh, sir...I had to come back to town for my school records and saw that there was a meeting tonight. I wanted to come and warn you about the HOA guys." Brian's eyes had finally found the group of demonic beings preparing to attack. "But, ha ha...it, uh, looks like you already know about them." He waved a hand casually at them. "Hey, Lili. Looking good, huh? I guess burying golden idols everywhere wasn't enough for you, so it's time to recruit the residents for the HOA cult now?" He gestured with a flick of his black hair at the assembled homeowners, still catatonic at their seats. "I wondered if you ever realized one of your treasures went missing. I guess I should thank you for the nest egg, though; my mom and I bought the nicest little house a few towns over. And do you want to know the best part about it?" He leaned in toward Lili's flaming eyes and smiled. "No HOA."

Lili snarled at him, and Brian flinched. Will nudged him with an elbow, and Brian turned back. With a flick of his wrist Will opened an extendable baton—pulled from yet another pocket—flipped it over end to end, and handed it to Brian. "No pressure, but just in case you needed it." Brian took his place alongside his former neighbors as the horde descended.

Truth be told, Brian didn't help with the battle very much. But on the other hand, he didn't die either; he figured Batman would have approved. Will and Ellie danced among the monsters as they attacked, hacking and slicing in quick, sharp movements. If anything came at Brian, he would duck and swing his metal baton. He did connect several times, creating sounds of impact that were simultaneously satisfying and nauseating, because they all reminded him of the sound the idol had made bashing in his stepfather's skull.

It was over quickly, and silence fell once again in the rec center. Bodies and pieces of demons lay all over, and their blood puddled in places. The colors of gore ranged from blue to red to black, mixing together on the floor in swirls and streaks. Will and Ellie cleaned their weapons and sheathed them, then shared a kiss in the midst of the carnage. Will took a bottle out of yet another pocket and started sprinkling it around on the demon corpses. Ellie dug in one of her own pockets and pulled out a matchbook. At Will's nod, she lit one and dropped it onto Lili's prone form.

The bodies all went up at once, the blue flames burning cold and creating only the faintest wisps of smoke. The blood burned as well, and in less than a minute it was as if the Snowbridge HOA board had never existed. Only the presence of the glowing gem on the floor and the crowd of catatonic homeowners hinted at anything out of the ordinary. "Only one more thing left to do, kiddo," Will said, indicating the gem with a tilt of his head. Brian walked over to the gem, and with all his strength, he stomped on it. There was a bang and a flash, and the people from the meeting started to move and talk again as if nothing had happened. Their voices rose, confused but not exactly frightened. They had no idea what had just happened under their very noses.

Brian walked over to Will and Ellie, who each gave him a hug. He tried to hand the baton back to Will, who shook his head and said "Keep it. Keep practicing. Keep learning." He ruffled Brian's black hair in farewell, then he and Ellie slipped back out the side door from which they had come. Brian, of course, took the fire escape back up to the roof.

* * *

As the sun rose, Ellie taped up the last box and handed it to Will, who gave her a kiss and loaded it into the waiting truck. They had finally packed everything: the weaponry and the throwing targets, the guitars and the telescopes, and the mountains upon mountains of books.

Ellie leaned her back against the moving truck, crossing her arms and taking one last look at the house. "So, Rhode Island, then?"

Will tightened the last straps around their cargo and pulled the truck's rolling door closed. "Yes, indeed. Turns out that meteor shower had a little more oomph to it up there. An actual meteorite came down into a manmade lake near Woonsocket."

"You're joking. 'Woonsocket?'" Will nodded, his eyes twinkling. Ellie shrugged and dug into her pocket for the keys. "How many houses have they built so far around the lake?"

"Several dozen so far, with a few hundred more planned. There have already been a few strange occurrences there, and they say the HOA fees are killer."

"I bet they are." They squared off, each cupping a fist with their other hand. On the count of three, Ellie threw scissors against Will's rock. "Aw, no! Best out of three?"

"Nope."

Resigned to her fate, Ellie tossed him the keys and climbed into the passenger seat. Will settled in next to her and started the truck. "I'll go easy on you this time, I promise. It's about an eight-hour drive there. I'll only make you stop at three Civil War battlefields."

"Two. And I get to pick the driving music."

He reached over and took her hand. "On to the next one, then?"

Ellie nodded and turned the volume up on the truck's stereo. "There's always another one out there, it seems."

Will lifted Ellie's hand to his lips and kissed it. "The Road goes ever on, as they say. I'm glad to follow it, so long as we can do it together."

As the truck rumbled over the bridge and out of the